I0445537

Tom Hubbard Is Dead

A Novel

Robert Price

Amherst, Massachusetts
SlipperySlopePress.com

This novel is a work of fiction. All characters appearing in this work are fictitious. Any resemblance to real persons, living or dead, is purely coincidental.

Copyright ©2011 by Robert Edwin Price

All rights reserved. Except for purposes related to a review, no part of this book may be reproduced in any form without the publisher's permission,

For sales and distribution contact:
Slippery Slope Press
P.O. Box 3612
Amherst, MA 01004

Email: Info@SlipperySlopePress.com
Website: SlipperySlopePress.com

ISBN: 978-0-9847003-0-1 (paperback)
ISBN: 978-0-9847003-2-5 (kindle)
ISBN: 978-0-9847003-1-8(ebook)
Library of Congress Control Number: 2011918718

Dedicated to my mother and father

&

Many thanks to my loving partner;
I couldn't have done it without her.

Tom Hubbard Is Dead

Prologue

Tikrit, Iraq, October 14, 2003

The *tat-tat-tat-tat* of an AK-47 leapt from the other side of a wall. Two men dove down as bullets chipped mortar off the building behind them. Silence, and then a second burst, this time from a different direction.

"Holy Christ. Hubbard! Hubbard's f'ckin' hit!"

A geyser of blood shot straight up from Tom Hubbard's neck.

With bullets spraying the ground, sand seemed to explode underfoot and the men dealt as best they could. Scrambling, they dragged Hubbard's listless body behind what would have to pass, for now, as cover.

Hubbard, however, felt only calm. A comfortable snap had washed-out his vision and dismissed any immediate concerns for his patrol, or, in fact, for anything at all.

Another deafening onslaught sliced the air and kept the men pinned down. For Hubbard, these last thin sounds intermingled with darkness and he found himself back home in Newbury, walking with his sister toward the old family farmhouse as his mother waited at the door. Then, letting his sister's hand go, Tom shoved off from the dock and swam, ever so smoothly, into the black.

Chapter One

Stepping cautiously, collapsed umbrellas in hand, the mourners filed past rows of weathered headstones, making their way down the slippery slope of the burial ground's highest hill. The empty thud of car doors echoed off the neighboring houses, lower knolls and far concrete wall of the cemetery. Small American flags speckled the autumn landscape. Thick White Oaks held onto their last orange-brown leaves. Overhead, a few solitary sparrows darted about; dancing black dots against the gray sky. The news crews wrapped up their reports and the workers arrived to pack up the chairs and cover the pit. Tom Hubbard's gravesite emptied.

Trailing the other mourners, making his way down the hill, lanky Ted Dorsey turned for a final look at his old friend's grave and, taking his eyes off the path, tripped over a broken headstone.

"That was beautiful," he said, stumbling to regain his balance. "A real hero's send off."

"Right." Glancing over his shoulder, Neil Bingham rotated his portly upper body and shook his head at Ted's clumsiness. "Really brought the whole thing to, you know, closure."

"He called us in January. Told us that he was going

back over," Ted said. "But I still can't believe ... I was shocked when we found out that ... I never could picture Tom in the Army in the first place."

"Never mind a Lieutenant." Cigarette smoke rolled out of Neil's mouth. Swallowing hard, he battled an unsettled lump of emotion that threatened to rise up from his stomach. It had first emerged when the white-gloved horn player blew Taps and the honor guard's Captain handed Tom's mother the triangulated coffin flag. Until then, Tom's death had seemed remote to Neil, as though it had nothing to do with him—like the war itself; it happened on the other side of the world.

Neil flicked his cigarette away with a snap and the butt landed in the middle of the narrow roadway just in time for a slow moving black limousine to roll over it.

Taking a deep breath, Ted's thin face tensed and his cheeks quivered. He glanced back up the hill toward the gravesite and, as two workers loaded chairs into the back of a pickup truck, thought about how much he loved his wife Shelly.

Searching deep in his pants pockets, he fished for the car remote and keys. "That was his sister back from California. Did you recognize her?"

"What a dress." Neil watched Ted dig for the keys and now had a chance, the first since Ted had picked him up at Logan Airport that morning, to really look at his old high school friend.

Ted's once wiry body had solidified, and his head, which used to bounce around like a bobble-head on a spring, now cocked permanently forward as if he suffered from chronic sleeplessness.

"I noticed that Tom's cousin Tony ballooned out some," Neil said, well aware that his own once-youthful athletic build was also gone; his neck packed weight and almost hid his shirt collar and red tie's Windsor knot.

"Was Tony's sister there?"

"Melanie? No." Ted looked down at the wet tips of his cold and uncomfortable feet. He should have worn boots. Shelly, however, had laid out these shoes along with a suit the night before, the same time she had laid out her own clothes for the funeral. But at the last minute her father reneged on an offer to baby-sit the children, forcing her to stay home.

Ted made a half-moon with his right hand on the car's windshield and, leaning forward, peered in to check if the keys were in the ignition.

"If it's a remote," Neil huffed, losing his patience, "and if you had left it in the car, then you couldn't have locked us out."

Ted looked down at his shoes again

Neil looked up at the sky. "We're going to the wake, right?"

"The reception?"

"Whatever."

One by one, a procession of cars politely inched along the narrow cemetery road before disappearing behind a hill. A light drizzle started.

"You got the keys or what?"

Ted rummaged one more time through the pockets of his slacks. And then, finally, as if searching in a foreign place, put a hand in his suit jacket pocket and found the remote and keys.

"I hate suits," he said, pushing the little red button on the device.

They climbed into the car and joined the line of traffic slowly snaking through the cemetery, out the wrought iron gate, towards the other side of town to Tom Hubbard's memorial reception.

Chapter Two

The phone rang. Melanie checked the clock—half past twelve. The funeral and the burial were most likely over. Either her younger brother Tony or cousin Billy Quinn were calling, once again, to say how important it is that she attend, at the very least, the memorial reception for her cousin Tom. The previous evening she had angrily refused Tony's invitation to accompany him to both events. It had been the third time he asked and her refusal was more out of spite for his bugging her than it was from the embarrassment she felt for having to depend on his support; the invitations were charity. Sure, she was thirty-eight and still alone. But she thought, *So what? I'm better off without a man.*

The phone continued to ring.

And it wasn't just Tony and Billy. Her grieving aunt, too, since finding out about her son Tom's death, called Melanie multiple times and left long messages on the answering machine. The first messages the old woman left expressed a quiet sorrow over the loss of Tom while at the same time conveying a subtle concern for Melanie's wellbeing. Over the past two months, even before Tom's death, Melanie, feeling a need for privacy, had begun to avoid their weekly face-to-face check-ins and even their daily chitchat phone calls. She knew this troubled her aunt. But when Tom's burial date was set, and then as the date approached, the tone of her aunt's messages had turned into pleas for Melanie's attendance rather than a concern for Melanie's health and whereabouts. At one point, her aunt even coaxed her cousin Elizabeth—in town with her husband for her brother's funeral—to call Melanie and invite her to join the family in the front pews at the church, on the folding chairs at the gravesite and for the comfortable limousine ride from the church to the cemetery and then back to the house after the burial. Melanie had ignored Elizabeth's call as well.

However, even while rejecting all family invitations to attend the funeral, Melanie was still unsure about whether to go to the memorial reception. When Tony had originally asked if she planned to attend, Melanie gave him a vague, indefinite answer, wanting to keep all options open. There was, after all, one person who might show up whom she wanted to see.

The machine answered after the ninth ring. She waited for the outgoing message to finish and then turned up the volume.

"Hey, Mel, pick up. It's your brother, Tony. I know you're there. Pick up!" A pause. "Melanie, okay, so don't answer. Aunt Casey is driving me absolutely fuckin' nuts! She's acting like Tom's soul won't go to heaven unless you're there—Melanie!"

"Hi, Anthony."

"I knew you were home. Hope you're getting ready to go, 'cause Aunt Casey keeps asking me if I've talked to you. She's convinced you've locked yourself up in your house or something. You're coming, right?"

"Who was at the funeral?"

"Mel, whether you believe it or not, your family is

important. So get your shit together."

"Where are you?"

"I'm just leaving the cemetery now."

"Was it sad?"

"Mel."

"Did you get a limo ride?"

"Jesus Christ, Mel! Yes, it was sad. It was fucking horrible. You should have been there."

"Don't give me your shit, Anthony. Tell Aunt Casey I'll be there in about an hour."

"Thank God for that."

"See you later," she said. But she spoke to the dial tone. Her brother had already hung up.

Chapter Three

From a distance, the long limousine appeared to float over the dormant grass of the cemetery's grounds. It proceeded down a winding dirt road past the oppressive trunk of an old White Oak and then took a right before continuing along the paved road. Parked cars narrowed the way, slowing the limousine's pace to a crawl.

The day before, the local newspapers had printed, "In compliance with the military's request, the family wishes to keep the affair private." But then the same articles listed the place and time of both the funeral and burial. No one seemed to know how the information got in there. By that morning, word had circulated about town. So almost everyone who had ever met Tom or his family, and even those who hadn't but were simply curious, showed up at the church and later the gravesite.

Amazed at the size and make up of the crowd, Tom Hubbard's sister, Elizabeth, glowed like a prom queen. She looked out of the limousine's tinted windows at a pageant of her and her brother's contemporaries as they filtered down the cemetery hill to their cars. Overall, the morning had resembled a high school class reunion or a town fair, albeit a sad one. It seemed as though Newbury's entire populous had turned out to mourn her brother's death. Elizabeth felt she held up well under the weight of all the attention—superbly well. For her, the events of the morning passed in a splendid haze, similar to her wedding day.

Earlier that morning, at the end of the funeral, the newspaper reporters, freelance photographers, cable news crews with their vans and a crowd of devoted mourners assembled in the raw weather outside the church. The doors to the First Church of Newbury swung open. The assemblage parted as an honor guard wearing military dress uniforms carried out Tom's flag-draped coffin. Then Elizabeth stepped out from the small white church in her black, stylishly slim raincoat. A breeze caught the light material and slapped the garment open, revealing the sleek black dress underneath. Elizabeth thought she looked perfect. Staying one step ahead of her mother, she held onto the old woman's right arm. Her husband, Jon, conscientious and efficient, held Mrs. Hubbard's other arm. A cold, gray drizzle fell. Jon extended an umbrella to protect his mother-in-law's head. The short procession descended the church steps. News photographers jockeyed for the best position and took their shots as the soldier-pallbearers slid the coffin into the back of the hearse. Elizabeth, her mother and Jon had a clear path to the waiting limousine. The cameras then turned on them. Elizabeth ran her fingers through her straight black hair to show off the near-perfect make-up job on which she had spent hours. She heard the rapid, automatic click of camera shutters go off like machinegun fire. It was the most important she had ever felt in her life.

Now, after the burial, back in the limo, Elizabeth grew excited again. "There's Neil Bingham, Mother. And, oh, Ted Dorsey. I wonder if Julian Reynolds came? I used to have the biggest crush on him." Elizabeth cracked a smile and nudged her husband Jon.

"Tom would be so happy they came," Mrs. Hubbard responded, sounding distant, distracted. "I begged Tony to call Melanie again. I so hope she comes to the house."

"Mother, Melanie will do what Melanie will do. She always does."

Though Mrs. Hubbard had successfully controlled the temptation to resort to tears throughout the morning, her eyes were glazed, red and tired. Her attention drifted across the cemetery landscape. "Do you think Tom will get one of those? Those little flags? Do veterans put them there?"

The limousine stopped and started and stopped and started. Cars pulling into the procession from the side of the road afforded the long black vehicle no position of prominence. After a pensive pause, Mrs. Hubbard reflected aloud, "I met the most wonderful little boy up there. He had blonde hair and blue eyes and for a second he reminded me of your brother when he was little. Tom was such a beautiful baby. The boy's mother, though ..." Mrs. Hubbard's voice trailed off. Medication left her mind foggy and she had trouble finishing thoughts.

"My feet are freezing!" Elizabeth pounded her feet on the carpeted floor of the limousine. "What about the boy's mother?" she asked out of obligation.

"She seemed hurried ... but nice." Mrs. Hubbard's thoughts moved aimlessly. "The service was ... And Father Hilliard was ... Your father would have been so ..."

"Freezing!" Elizabeth abruptly kicked off one black pump and reached down to rub her toes. "You'd think these limos would have floor heat."

"For the life of me, Lizzy, I don't know why you wore those things anyway," Jon scolded.

The past few days had worn on Jon, dropping things the way they had to fly across the country to attend to

Mrs. Hubbard and the funeral arrangements. First, he had to take care of his caseload at the firm. That was relatively simple; as a senior partner he had confidence in several of the junior partners. If they had questions, they knew to call him. He could be easily reached by cell. Next, while Elizabeth was making flight arrangements and canceling her various appointments and engagements around the Valley, he arranged for his mother to take care of their two children. Thankfully, she was more than happy to spend time with the grandchildren. She would have them for Shabbat and bring them to synagogue.

Then there was the difficulty at the airport. The name "Jon Goldberg" sent up a security flag. It appeared that some "Jon Goldberg" somewhere, at some point in time, had done something to threaten America's security. So his name had landed on the nation's No Fly list. Upon check-in, plain-clothes security officials appeared out of nowhere and whisked Jon away from Elizabeth's side. For over an hour he answered questions about his relationship with his brother-in-law, Tom, whom he had met only once on his and Elizabeth's wedding day. The dutiful security officers needed to check out his story. After all, he was flying to Boston, the birthplace of 9/11. The officers remained unfazed when Jon tried his lawyerly best to explain that the purpose of his trip to Massachusetts was to bury, not visit, his brother-in-law who was, in fact, a casualty of the war. Finally the officers, satisfied with their security check, let Jon go. And at the last moment, as the flight attendant was closing the aircraft's door, Jon slipped through and joined Elizabeth in first class. Now, heading back to the farmhouse in the limousine, imagining that the bulk of this long day had already passed, he loosened his tie.

"Oh, please, Jon. Those boots are no warmer than

these shoes." Elizabeth continued rubbing her toes. "I still can't get over all the people. Do you think we should call the caterer and let them know we're on our way? Mother?"

Rain pattered on the tinted windows. "Lizzy, your father would have been so proud. He was proud of both of you, at times. Father Hilliard said it was your father's pride that killed him. But, well, all this, all these people. Your father went to Korea. I never thought Tom would have to fight, too ..."

"Mother," Elizabeth leaned forward and placed a hand softly on the elderly woman's knee. She looked intently at the side of her mother's face and wondered if her own cheeks would sag like that when she got older. Her mother's hair seemed grayer now than it had that morning. Perhaps it was the grayness of the day or the tinted windows. Elizabeth made the decision right then and there that she would dye her hair long before it turned so colorless. Mrs. Hubbard placed a hand lovingly on top of Elizabeth's. Elizabeth squinted, examining the red lipstick that formed a crooked ridgeline along her mother's mouth and followed wrinkles that crept like vines from the edge of the old woman's lips to the rest of her face. Her mother had had a hard life.

Elizabeth sat back in her seat. "Jon, do you mind calling them? Just give 'um a buzz and let them know we are on our way."

Jon took out his cell phone. "I think I may still have the number."

Mrs. Hubbard spoke quietly, as if from far away, "You've been so good, Jon. I wish the children could have come as well." Her gaze followed the fluctuating tree line that bordered the cemetery.

Jon nodded and smiled, acknowledging his mother-in-law's compliment. Although he tried to play the role of the dutiful son-in-law, he hardly ever spoke directly to her. Mrs. Hubbard's emotional instability reminded him too much of his own father's battle with depression. Jon's father had lumbered for years between being half asleep and half angry, a depressed Dr. Jekyll-Mr. Hyde personality. His poor father would obsess for hours over seemingly small, inconsequential things. Some days, a broken pencil tip was enough to send the man to tears and little Jon to his bedroom for punishment. Finally, psychotropic medications offered his father, and thus Jon and his mother, short spans of relief from the unpredictability of mental illness. But the man needed to take the medication for it to work. Mrs. Hubbard suffered from this problem as well. Since Jon and Elizabeth's arrival in Newbury, Elizabeth's constant questioning of, "Has she taken her medication?" left him feeling as unsafe as he had around his own father. In fact, Jon almost expected an episode, a breakdown, like the one that had happened at their wedding and had landed Mrs. Hubbard in the hospital. This was her only son's funeral, after all. If Elizabeth thought calling the caterer would help to keep her mother from dissolving, Jon was only too happy to assist.

"Mother," Elizabeth leaned forward, trying to draw her mother's gaze away from the window. "I really think you should ..." Exasperated with the lack of response, Elizabeth shook her mother's knee, "Mother! Please listen."

"Oh, I'm sorry, dear." Mrs. Hubbard finally turned from the landscape to her daughter. "I just can't help but think how he would have enjoyed this."

"I really think you should try to take it easy today at the reception. If even only a few of these people show up at the house, it's going to be very crowded."

"I wished he hadn't publicly announced it like that,"

Jon said, cell phone pressed to an ear. "I mean, really, couldn't the priest have at least been a bit more discreet about the whole thing? Ahh, hello, is this Arnaldo?" With a free hand, Jon swatted at an invisible communication problem. "This is Jon Goldberg. Yes, all went well. What? How many people? Well, do your best. We are on our way. Thank you." He snapped the phone shut and let out a breath. "It seems some folks have beaten us to the house. Arnaldo says cars are already parking out front. But nobody has come in yet. He's all set up—buffet, booze, everything."

"Many cars?" Elizabeth asked.

"I don't know. I have trouble understanding him— his accent. I just hope it's not too many. Still, I wish the priest hadn't announced it like that."

"I asked him to."

"Mother?"

"Yesterday morning, after you arranged things, he called and asked what I thought. I told him to invite everyone. I said, 'Invite them all, to everything ... the funeral, burial and the reception. Tom would love it.'"

"You mean Father Hilliard called you after we left and asked if he could tell the whole world?" Elizabeth realized then that the priest had disregarded her directives and gone behind her back to double-check with her mother. "Bastard."

Elizabeth and Jon had specifically told the old priest to honor the military's request that Tom's funeral and graveside ceremony be kept private. They had also told the priest that the memorial reception at the farmhouse was intended to give extended family, older friends and anyone with a valid connection to Tom an opportunity to pay their respects to the immediate family in an intimate setting. Elizabeth had envisioned the reception as a personal and purposeful gathering; not a wake, but more like a baptism or confirmation.

"So let me get this straight? It was Father Hilliard who told the reporters, the newspapers and the TV stations about the funeral and the burial? Jesus, Mother, they asked us to keep those quiet—just family and friends. Now, after that announcement, the memorial reception, too—" Elizabeth shook her head with distain. "Now everybody is going to be there."

Outwardly frustrated, Elizabeth gave up and pushed back into the plush seat of the limousine. Secretly, however, she looked forward to remaining the central figure of the day.

Chapter Four

The old farmhouse on Quinns Way looked smaller, more worn-out than the one in the childhood photos Tom had shown him. Ezekiel examined the neglected structure, unsure of what made the place appear so different. Was it the absence of the sepia colored fields that had surrounded the house in Tom's photographs? Or was it the newer houses behind the Hubbard house, with their fences, trees, manicured shrubbery and smooth driveways, which made the old place, situated high on a rise of land, look more like a relic than a livable house? Either way, the peeling, white-painted, two-story building with the strange yet formal portico that jutted out of the front appeared much smaller than Ezekiel had expected. Smaller, anyway, than the youthful exaggerations Tom had shared with him over intimate dinners or casual, long Sunday afternoon walks.

Studying the rundown farmhouse now, in the dismal, gray daylight, Ezekiel felt even more distant from his partner than during the funeral or the burial. Looking at the old place through the rain-spotted windshield of the rented car produced a hollow feeling in him, a feeling that resembled a loss of faith, or hope, or even dreams. It was a feeling that Ezekiel, at forty-five years old, thought he was far too young to experience.

He watched as other mourners parked and then walked up the long, circular driveway.

On the passenger's seat, Ezekiel had placed a small knapsack full of memorabilia, photographs that he hoped to share with Tom's family. He reached for the bag and pulled out a picture of Tom and himself standing arm in arm, wearing funky Hawaiian shirts on a beach in Puerto Rico—their first trip together. Right beneath was another photo Ezekiel had taken the morning before Tom last reported for active duty. There was Tom, handsome and trim in his desert fatigues, still blonde at thirty-seven, unshaven and mocking the camera, his square jaw protruding as he stood in their kitchen holding a frying pan as if it were an assault rifle. The next photo featured Tom and Ezekiel on the front lawn of their small house in Arlington, Virginia. It was taken shortly after they had purchased the place. Tom jokingly cradled the "For Sale" sign like a baby in his arms.

Using his index finger, Ezekiel traced Tom's image over the clear plastic sleeve that protected the photograph. *He was a beautiful man.* Tom had meant the world to him.

Tears filled his eyes as the long black limousine that carried Tom's family rolled by and turned up the curve of the driveway. People who had waited outside for the family's arrival now stepped back, creating an aisle that led under the portico to the front door. The rise of the unkempt lawn and the standing crowd obstructed his view somewhat, but Ezekiel, even from where his car was parked on the road's shoulder, could still see well enough. The tears flowed harder as he waited for his partner's family to step out of the limousine. He had never even met them.

Earlier in the day, when the family was leaving the church, Ezekiel had struggled with the emotional burden that went along with honoring Tom's decision to keep their relationship a secret from his family. From a distance, Ezekiel had watched the family descend the church steps. Mrs. Hubbard was in the middle, Elizabeth in the forefront, Jon a step behind with an umbrella. They appeared to be supporting Mrs. Hubbard, holding her up by the arms. As he watched, questions plagued Ezekiel: *Shouldn't I be helping her? Wasn't I the closest to her son? Wasn't it my job as her son's partner to be next to her in that procession?*

Then, as the television cameras receded and the hearse pulled away from the church with the family's limousine following closely behind, Ezekiel's feelings shifted and he felt the weight of guilt. *Am I responsible for Mrs. Hubbard losing her son? After all, wasn't I the one who had kissed Tom goodbye the morning he reported for active duty? Shouldn't I have tried harder to influence Tom to refuse to go? Convince him to go AWOL? Become a Conscientious Objector?*

Later, at the gravesite, instead of asking himself fruitless questions, Ezekiel yearned for the family's acceptance. During the burial ceremony he admired his should-be mother-in-law. She stood stolidly in black—the proud, grieving mother of a fallen hero. Taps played, and tucked under her arm was the triangle of the folded American flag from her son's coffin. Ezekiel wished he could stand next to her and be included in her thoughts and feelings, as she was in his.

Now, after the ride from the gravesite to the Hubbard Farmhouse, parked in his rented car across the street, Ezekiel watched Elizabeth and Jon as they stood beside the limousine under the portico by the front door of the house. They turned to greet the visitors. And although Ezekiel could only see them from their shoulders up—Elizabeth's black hair and manicured features, and Jon's dark hair and the shadow of his heavy eyebrows—Ezekiel was struck by how similar the scene appeared to a photo Tom had shown him of his sister's wedding seven years earlier. Even though it had been impossible for them to invite Ezekiel—because Tom had never even told them that he existed—he was the one, not Tom, who had bought the newlyweds the set of fancy carving knives and then had the knife handles engraved with their wedding date. Tom had only delivered the gift. And over the years it was he, not Tom, who sent the congratulation cards and flowers upon the births of Elizabeth and Jon's children. It was also he, not Tom, who entered the children's birthdates into a date book every year and faithfully got Tom to sign and mail a card along with a small gift. And it was he, not Tom, who proudly hung Elizabeth and Jon's family holiday photo on the refrigerator each year, and lovingly mailed one of Tom in return.

When Mrs. Hubbard emerged from the limousine, Ezekiel's eyes grew wide and he had to gulp down a tear. He had not noticed it before; maybe she hadn't worn it earlier? Mrs. Hubbard had wrapped a black shawl around her shoulders and covered her head with it like a hood. Ezekiel could clearly see the shawl's distinct and familiar gold fringe. He had picked out that shawl himself, paid for it and brought it home for Tom to send to his mother. At the time, Tom was tense, distracted, preoccupied with the pressure of returning to the war. Ezekiel remembered their argument about the gift and how Tom had told him to butt out of his family matters, that his mother didn't need another shawl. Ezekiel, however, was determined that he knew better. In the end, Ezekiel got his way, and, as usual, Tom signed his name on the card.

The day before Tom left for the war, Ezekiel wrapped the shawl and shipped it in time for Mrs. Hubbard's last birthday.

Now, seeing the shawl wrapped around Mrs. Hubbard's shoulders, Ezekiel grew angry at having agreed with Tom to keep their partnership a secret from this family. He cared about these people, yet they remained clueless to his very existence. Now, with Tom gone, he longed for their acceptance and support. *It isn't fair. I was the one, not Tom, who had kept contact with this family. Why should I be forced to be so alone today?*

He watched as Mrs. Hubbard held on to Elizabeth and Jon's hands as they guided her through the small crowd and into the farmhouse.

Hidden in his car, Ezekiel felt like some big, black, gay freak who loved this little white family.

Chapter Five

Julian Reynolds decided, once again, to pack in his dreams. Just give up his online art gallery and get a real job. None of it had panned out the way he envisioned. Instead of making a living by selling his inexpensive giclee prints—reproductions of his watercolor paintings, matted, mounted and shrink-wrapped in several standard frame sizes—he found that he was barely scrapping by. Over the past two years he had moved boxes and piles of prints around the small, one bedroom apartment more than actually moving individual pieces out the door. The last time he sold and shipped a print was over three months ago. It was of a waterfall in Jamaica, Vermont, and it went to a friend of his mother. Thirty-nine years old and his parents had paid the rent for the last seven months.

It was 12:30 p.m. and Julian, still shaky from drinking the night before, walked around the crowded living room that also served as an office and storage space. He bumped into a stack of open boxes and knocked a pile of prints to the floor—autumn colors surrounding a maple syrup shack.

"How many of these fucking things did I have made?" Julian's stomach tightened with impending sickness as he bent over to pick up the prints. He paused to let the feeling pass, then collected the pictures and, standing up slowly, placed them back in their box. His stomach wrestled with the morning, but he reminded himself, "It will pass."

Sitting on the couch, he tried to focus on the day. He had missed Tom Hubbard's funeral, and probably the graveside ceremony, but maybe there was still time to make the memorial reception at the Hubbard's old house. On the floor lay a plastic half-gallon bottle of vodka. Picking the bottle up and holding his breath, he took a long drink. With chest muscles tightening and he waited. Once sure the vodka would stay down, he pushed a hand through his oily hair. "Should I shower? Do I have the time?" He looked around at the wasteland of cardboard boxes and piles of prints and then glanced over to the computer.

The maintenance of his website suffered. Every time he went online to check for sales or inquiries he ended up on porn sites and masturbating instead. The screen had turned into a twenty-one-inch sexual trigger. Lately, he found himself completely enamored by she-male sites. One page in particular featured three women with perfect breasts and long dicks and kept him busy fantasizing for hours on end. When he refrained from masturbating or had a brief respite from drinking, Julian would sit at the computer, smoke cigarettes and review the shambles of his life—divorce, an inability to make a living, debt. All of it amounted to failure.

"No, I'll wash and go."

In the shower he looked down at his protruded liver and hated himself. "Shit, I look like hell." The hot water and perfumed soap stung his dry skin.

After, Julian stood naked in the middle of his living, office and storage room wondering what to wear. By then his morning drink had begun to kick in and the alcohol momentarily transformed his self-image. "No, I'll be alright," he thought aloud. "After all, I'm a fucking Artist. I have my own online gallery ... a fucking art gallery. Shit, some would even say I'm successful; I'm not a pathetic 9-to-5er. I do what I want, when I want ..."

Suddenly proud, hands on hips, like the hero of a battle, he surveyed the mess: half-eaten sandwiches; empty, plastic half-gallon bottles; and dangerously full ashtrays that intermingled with the boxes and piles of prints.

The answering machine's red message light winked from under an ashtray. The previous morning he had shut off the phone's ringer and turned the contraption's volume down after a collection agent called with threats. Upon hanging up on the pesky woman, he drank some until slipping into oblivion. Now, the next day, feeling more courageous, he moved a print—an old mill building covered with snow—out of the way of the "play message" button and, turning the volume up, heard his mother's distinct Southern accent. "You must know by now, well, I would think you'd know, that your old high school friend, Tom Hubbard, was killed in action in Iraq. We didn't even know he was over there. Did you tell us? Anyway, I'm so sorry to hear. I hope you are okay. Call us, Julian. We love you."

Julian turned the volume down again. "Fucking mother, how'd she know? What was it, broadcast in Florida?"

He took another long drink from the bottle, almost finishing it.

Leaning over, touching the computer keyboard, the monitor's black screen sprang from hibernation and filled with the image of a person, half-man and half-woman, legs spread apart, crotch bulging and lips wanting. He paused and then clicked to his home page to check the clock. "I gotta get outta here."

But the image of the man-woman lingered in his thoughts. Clicking back, the she-male once again filled the screen. A tingling sensation flickered around the tip of his penis. Shame washed over him as he realized it was the same picture he had ogled over three days earlier when Melanie, Tom's cousin, had called to share the bad news. He was half-drunk when answering her call at 8:30 in the morning. His pants were around his ankles, his penis erect in hand. Then he proceeded to flirt while she tried to inform him of Tom's death.

"What are you wearing?" He had emphasized his soft Southern accent that he knew she liked.

Although Melanie had not discouraged his manor, she stopped short of encouraging him. She simply listened to the flirtatious comments and then told him about the funeral arrangements and memorial reception.

After their conversation, after hanging up the phone, he actually stopped to think about Tom. He hoped that Tom had died quickly. Making a rare entry into his empty calendar book to note the time of the funeral, he then returned to satisfying himself without giving Melanie or Tom another thought. Until now.

Ashamed of his behavior that morning when she had called, Julian sighed; Melanie would be there today, at Tom's memorial reception.

Chapter Six

The blue sweater brought out her eyes. The yellow sweater made her face appear pleasantly flushed. But the brown sweater fit snug and made her look alluring. This was the sweater that would turn some heads and perhaps land her in conversations instigated for no other reason than to flirt. Melanie tucked her black hair behind her ears. Pushing her shoulders back, her breasts firmly rose up under the tight sweater. "There. Perfect."

In the mirror, Melanie could see over her shoulder and out the window. As a girl, and up until recently, that is before the acreage across the street sold, she had loved this particular reflection: In one view, she could see both her own face and the landscape—the road, the fields leading down to Parker River, the tree-lined river bank and beyond that, the hills of her hometown, Newbury.

But that pastoral landscape was gone now.

Melanie leaned closer to the mirror and smoothed her dark eyebrows. Out of the corner of her eye, and in the image of the window in the mirror, she watched a pickup truck wobble down a muddy makeshift driveway to the waiting foundation of the third house being built in the old field across the street. For some reason, when she had sold the field two years earlier, she never imagined that they would actually build on it.

At least I'm not as crazy as Auntie Casey, selling her land to that other even greedier builder. She smoothed the front of her sweater. *Fifteen houses in a cul-de-sac!*

Melanie's aunt, Mrs. Hubbard, was her mother's sister. These two sisters, with the maiden name of Quinn, were from one of the oldest families in town. In 1635, a young Puritan ancestor from Boston named Samuel Quinn paddled up Plum Island Sound with a handful of settlers to found the town of Newbury, Massachusetts. Since then, and until the Second World War, it seemed that either a Quinn or a Quinn relative owned most of the farmland around Newbury. Those days had passed. But still, Melanie's mother, her aunt and cousin Billy's father, Uncle William, each inherited sizable sections of the Quinn Farm when Melanie's grandfather had died. Uncle William, the oldest, inherited the bulk of the farm. Aunt Casey, Mrs. Hubbard, the oldest daughter, inherited the family farmhouse and the haying fields, plus a smaller field along Quinns Way. Much to Mrs. Hubbard's husband Edward's chagrin, she deeded that field to Tom shortly after his birth.

Wonder what will happen to that last piece of land Auntie Casey had saved for Tom, Melanie thought as she slid on her shoes. *It's gotta be worth a bundle now.*

Melanie's mother, Barbara, the youngest Quinn of that generation, inherited the leftover property, the pieces below Old Town Hill and toward the Parker River. Then Melanie's mother married Eugene Griffin, a man from another old Newbury farming family. The Griffins had a history of difficulties—alcohol, gambling and debts—that kept them from holding onto their land. Even with those losses, however, when Melanie's mother married her father, they combined their landholdings and ended up with close to twenty acres, not enough to farm for a living, but not bad for 1960's Newbury either. When Melanie and her brother Tony's parents died—their father from drinking and their mother shortly thereafter from breast cancer—the bulk of the property went to Tony, the oldest male in the family. Like her mother had before her, Melanie got the leftovers; the old Griffin family house and four acres, three of which she had sold two years ago and were now being built upon.

Melanie turned to face the window and sighed at the sight of the new construction. She pulled the shade down and gave herself a short pep talk: "So what if they build. Tony and Billy were right—it was smart of me to sell that land. And like they said, I still have this place. Besides ..." she said, turning back to the mirror, "I look great!" Satisfied, she now turned to survey the room and thought, *I wonder if he'll show up?*

Although she felt that Julian had been out of line when she called to explain about Tom's death—flirting the way he did—still, she blushed at the thought. She had always had a crush on him.

Melanie's first memory of Julian was from ninth grade English class, when their tyrannical teacher, Mrs. Arnbuckel, scolded him for poking her cousin Tom in the back with a pencil. Julian, with dorky glasses and a flowery Southern-accent, was the new kid in town. As punishment for poking Tom and disrupting the class, Mrs. Arnbuckel brought Julian to the front of the room and had him read a Robert Frost poem aloud. When he read, Julian exaggerated his Southern accent to sound like a backwoods hillbilly. "Two roads diverge in a yeller ward." Melanie fell for him right then and there.

She re-checked the sheets on the bed and smoothed a quilt over them.

Ten years ago, when Tom told her that Julian had

married a foreign woman in a foreign country, she secretly hoped their marriage would fail. Then, five years later, she hosted a big Christmas party. Tom, who was visiting from Arlington, Virginia, and considering a move back to the Boston area, came to the party and invited his old high school friends, too. Julian arrived without his wife. Melanie made a move on him and drunkenly took him to bed that night. Two years ago, around the same time she had quit drinking alcohol, she heard that Julian's wife had left him. Melanie called under the pretext of consoling him. That night began a series of long, sometimes quite personal, phone conversations—conversations that led nowhere.

The other morning, however, when she called to tell him about Tom's death, she heard a genuine longing in his flirtatious voice. After he asked what she was wearing—and after she ignored the question—he whispered that he remembered the scent of her perfume.

Melanie touched a fingertip of rose oil behind each ear before returning the small, round glass bottle to the top of the dresser. Her cell phone chirped from under a pile of folded clothes on the chair next to the bed. *Julian?* She had asked him to call with his plans. But he hadn't. *He's an artist,* she reasoned. *They're all a little flakey.* Unfamiliar with the number on the caller ID, she picked up the cell phone and, flipping her hair back, answered singing, "Hello, this is Mel."

"Mel, why are you still home?" her cousin, Billy Quinn, yelled.

She held the phone away from her ear. "Billy, where are you calling from?" Both Billy and his wife, Jeannine, annoyed her. And she thought they spoiled their three young daughters.

"We're just turning up Quinns Way now."

On the other hand, Melanie knew Billy and Jeannine

felt a sense of responsibility toward her, and that was helpful at times. Since the death of her mother, shortly after graduating from high school, Billy, Jeannine and Melanie's brother, Tony, had watched with fear as Melanie slowly descended into the isolated and unmanageable life of an alcoholic. They bailed her out of jail after being arrested for fighting with another woman in a bar. They hired lawyers to defend her in court in a drunken driving case. And when she finally lost her license for over a year for a second DUI conviction, they shared the burden of carting her around town when she needed a ride. Later, it was Billy and Tony who found her at the end of her last binge, hiding in her upstairs bedroom, unable to function, afraid to descend the stairs, surrounded by empty bottles and pots and pans full of her own pee. They dragged her to Baldpate Hospital for detox. And when she was finally dried out, it was Billy and Tony who sifted through her affairs and discovered the financial wreckage. They convinced her that her debts were so extreme that the only way to pay her back taxes, keep the old house and hold onto a bit of family heritage was to sell the land across the street.

"Whose phone is this?" If she had known it was going to be Billy, she would have let it ring. Now sober for two years, she was tired of him always watching over her.

"It's Jeannine's, for Christ's sake. Listen, are you coming or what?"

"I'm just leaving. Did you bring the kids with you?"

"No, Jeannine's parents are bringing them by later. We didn't want them at the funeral."

Melanie heard Jeannine gasp in the background.

"Holy shit ..." Billy swerved his huge silver pickup to avoid hitting a woman who was reaching into the open back door of her car. He drove straight through a deep puddle and sent a spray of water flying in the woman's direction.

"What happened?"

"You'll be there, right?" Billy barked, issuing an order.

"I'm leaving riii ..."

Without waiting for an answer he snapped his phone shut.

This was another reason why Melanie tried to avoid Billy's calls. Like Tony, he would call, tell her what to do, and then hang up. The hopeful mood she had enjoyed before the call now sank. She hated being treated like one of his employees. His voice ringing in her ear—*You'll be there, right?*—awakened her insecurities as well as a feeling of guilt for having avoided her aunt, both during the past months and now, most recently, in the days after Tom's death. She would go to the house and face her aunt, stomach full of butterflies. As she pulled on a tweed blazer, she felt like a nervous actor called out to center stage.

Chapter Seven

The splash from a passing pickup truck soaked the back of Carrie Phillips's skirt. She remained unfazed however and, ignoring the driver's inconsiderate ways, stayed focused on the task at hand. Keeping one foot on the street for balance, she stretched her body through the back door of the small car and struggled to undo a stubborn snap on the harness of her son's car seat. She tried to remain calm while wrestling with the clasp, yet her son had an alternative plan. The boy, using his tiny fingers, noodled at the pile of crimson-colored curly hair on the top of her head. Suddenly, the fidgety child had had it with waiting and he tugged on a single curl. "Tommy, please," she tried to hide her annoyance. The boy's lips began to tremble. Sensing his impending tears, she leaned in further to better grip the strap and the clasp. Her foot slipped on the wet pavement and she inadvertently tightened instead of loosening the harness around the boy's chest. This sudden discomfort provided the excuse the boy needed and, interpreting the tug as punishment, Tommy burst into tears.

"Oh, Mother of God," Carrie said. "Please. I'm sorry, Tommy. Mommy didn't mean it. I know you're tired. Mommy's tired, too, but we'll only be here for a minute."

She brushed his blonde hair back from his forehead and kissed him on the cheek.

"There, there," she said, succeeding in freeing the child.

The boy climbed down from the car seat, crawled across the back seat of the car and then lowered himself onto the pavement. He rubbed his damp cheeks.

"Will you be a big boy for Mommy when we get inside?"

The boy looked up at his mother, blinked his blue eyes and confidently nodded his head up and down.

Chapter Eight

Ezekiel wiped the dampness that hung under his eyes with a tissue: *Am I presentable?* Peering into the car's rearview mirror to check his face, he spotted coming up the road, a short, petite woman dressed in a long skirt and a cropped leather jacket with a pile of curly hair on the top of her head. A half step behind, a cute little boy rubbed his eyes with one hand and held onto the woman's hand with his other. Ezekiel's heavy heart lifted and he smiled at their image in the mirror. *A colorful couple,* he thought. So colorful, they resembled animated paper cutouts walking past what appeared to be the last undeveloped stretch of empty, gray farmland on the street. He laughed out loud watching the reluctant boy stop in the middle of the road, forcing the calm yet determined woman to more or less tow the child. Snapping his jacket collar up around his neck and climbed out of the car to join the pair on their walk to the house.

"Looks like you've caught yourself a live one there." Ezekiel offered a big smile. His dark skin made his white teeth shine. A tall, large man, he waved an energetic and big *hello*. People liked Ezekiel, and Ezekiel knew it.

"It seems like you have your job cut out for you with

that one," Ezekiel spoke again, this time with deliberate warmth; he knew he was in a mostly white community. Except for the camera crews outside of the church after the funeral, the only black face he'd seen all day was his own in the mirror. He walked around the car to the passenger's side, but instead of picking up the knapsack of memorabilia, he suddenly changed his mind and tugged the door handle as if checking the lock.

"Him?" Carrie smiled. "He's a fine one, this one." Picking up on Ezekiel's invitation to talk, she stopped walking. Her long, damp skirt swayed and then stuck to the back of her legs. Carrie pulled the fabric free.

Little Tommy came to a standstill. "Mommy's behind got wet."

"Shhhh." Carrie kneeled in front of her son and fixed his short, clip-on tie and little sports jacket. "He doesn't need to know about Mommy's skirt, Tommy. Let's keep that our little secret," she said, kissing him on the cheek.

"It is a wet day and that cemetery grass was slippery." Ezekiel crossed the street to join them.

"No," Carrie answered kindly. After having spent the morning explaining incomprehensible things, like soldiers and cemeteries to a five-year-old, she was glad to converse with an adult. "It was a puddle and a pickup truck." She extended her hand to Ezekiel: "I'm Carrie, and this little man is Tommy."

"Tommy! My pleasure to make your acquaintance, Tommy." Ezekiel spoke in a deep, happy voice, and like a genie that had emerged in a puff of smoke from its bottle, he pounded his chest with his fist: "My name is Ezekiel." He held up his hand as if just completing a magic trick.

Little Tommy, delighted, liked Ezekiel instantly.

The older man bowed to the boy and laughed a big laugh.

"That was wonderful!" Carrie exclaimed, laughing with him.

"Oh, a little comic relief on such a sad day is good for the soul." As Ezekiel spoke, he gently guided Carrie and Tommy to the side of the road just as a small green sedan passed. "We don't want a repeat performance."

"No, not today. No more puddles today. I think I'm wet enough."

Tommy reached for his mother's hand and then the three of them together faced the farmhouse. They proceeded slowly, cautiously, up the driveway toward the crowd that gathered under the portico, uncertain of what lay ahead.

Chapter Nine

Ted and Neil found themselves at the tail end of a long line of vehicles that weaved across town from the cemetery to the Hubbard farmhouse. When they finally arrived, they found two large pickup trucks and an SUV practically blocking the intersection of Hay Street and Quinns Way. Parked with their rear ends in the middle of the road, they made it impossible for Ted Dorsey to take the turn safely. Unable to see past the vehicles, he tightly gripped the steering wheel of his small green sedan and crept around the corner, hoping he wouldn't hit anyone who might be walking down the road.

"This area has sure changed, huh?" Neil had already made this comment several times since they had turned off High Road and cut through the parking lot of Hutchin Farm & Market to get to Hay Street.

"So the Hubbards sold most of it, except this piece?" Neil said, referring to a rare open field they were passing. "Wow."

He then pointed to the new development built directly opposite it. A whole neighborhood had been constructed where the old haying fields used to be. "Those new places back right up to the road? Those are their backyards on the other side of the fence?"

A new post and rail fence ran the length of Quinns Way and disappeared behind the rise on which the Hubbard farmhouse stood. Except for the old Sugar Maples lining the street, the new fence was the only thing that hinted at the historically rural character of the area. It was supposed to conjure up images of open farmland. But instead, the new neighborhood, with its younger ornamental trees, children's wooden play sets, above-ground swimming pools and the dauntingly large, newly-built colonial houses complete with two-car garages made the bucolic illusion just that, an illusion.

"You enter those neighborhoods off Green Street, by the end of the old haying fields," Ted said. "There was a big to-do in the newspaper about leaving Quinns Way intact. So they put up that fence. I think the town's historic commission required it." Ted was more concerned with parking than he was with telling Neil about the sale and development of the Hubbard's farmland, so he left it at that.

"Holy shit, Tom's house looks rundown," Neil said, squirming, his fat and bulky body uncomfortable in the small passenger's seat.

Ted slowed his green car as he passed a large man, a smaller woman and a sleepy looking child. "Well, you know, Mrs. Hubbard's been pretty much alone. The old man died, and Tom never visited, and his sister moved away right after high school. So there's only Tony and Melanie, Tom's cousins, and his other cousins, the Quinns. Other than that, it's just her." Ted pulled into the first open spot on the side of the road.

A brown, beat-up sedan with a bumper sticker that read, *"God is at the helm,"* pulled in front of them.

"How did I even fit into this thing?" Neil mumbled, spilling out of the small car onto the street. He discreetly pulled up on his belt and the back of his slacks.

Ted stretched his thin neck; ties bothered him. Collecting his thoughts, he got out of the car, locked the door and waved to the driver of the car that had parked in front of them. "Father Hilliard! I thought that was you."

Father Hilliard, an elder, balding man with colorless hair on the sides, turned around with a lost expression. He couldn't make out who had called. Although he couldn't see clearly beyond a couple of feet, the Father made it a habit to drive without glasses. Slowly he took a pair of bifocals from a breast pocket and pushed them over the bridge of his nose. Then adjusting a white tab-collar and black clergy shirt and looking toward Ted and Neil, he finally fiddled with his hearing aid. It took him a full minute to gather up all the available information. "Well, hello, Mr. Dorsey," Father Hilliard said at length.

"Hello, Father." Ted tried to speak in a somber tone, appropriate for the occasion. Instead his excitement revealed the honor felt at having stumbled upon the opportunity to escort the holy man to the gathering. After all, the old Priest had baptized not only him and Shelly, but their children also. He approached Father Hilliard with a hand extended. "Thank you, Father, for the lovely service at the cemetery."

Father Hilliard raised his bushy salt and pepper eyebrows in a practiced, kindly manner.

Neil nodded a quick hello to the priest and to his friend said, "I'll catch you inside." He started toward the house and then turned: "Hey, don't forget my flight outta here tonight."

"I know, I know. Logan Airport, American Airlines, 10:38 p.m."

"Thanks." Neil crossed the street and walked up the driveway to the farmhouse alone.

"How are you?" Father Hilliard searched his

parishioner's eyes, intending to let the younger man know he is willing to listen, that is, if a desire to share sorrow comes forth.

Ted spoke slowly and directly, compensating for Father Hilliard's poor hearing: "I'm doing well, Father, I'm doing well,"

"You two had been great friends since you were boys." Reaching up, Father Hilliard placed a hand on Ted's shoulder, letting it rest there. "If only we could live twice. But it was wise of the Lord to limit us to one life on earth, or else in our next lives we'd end up making the same mistakes over again."

"Yeah, we already do that in this one, don't we?"

"My boy, it would seem that way."

Slightly amused by Father Hilliard's comment, the two turned toward the house and proceeded to cross the street, unhurried.

"So, how is Shelly holding up? She seemed upset on Sunday."

"She's doing better. Stuck home with the kids ... Her father," Ted shook his head angrily, "he bailed on us again."

"We all do what we can, Ted. I'm sure he tried."

Several children had gathered under the portico and around the front of the house. The somber mood of the adults around them kept them from playing in the yard. However they did call out to Father Hilliard and Ted Dorsey in excited "Hellos."

"Shhh," Ted gently quieted the children. And to Father Hilliard he added, "I think I'm going to give Shelly a call and tell her to come on over with the kids."

"Good," Father Hilliard agreed. "I think we, as God's creatures, are naturally inclined to protect our children. But at times I think maybe we protect them too much. It would be nice to have the whole family here."

Ted Dorsey and Father Hilliard passed through the open front door and into the Hubbard farmhouse, shaking hands in the entrance hallway before going their separate ways. Ted headed to the dining room for a soda, Father Hilliard set off in search of Mrs. Hubbard.

Chapter Ten

Two days earlier, the morning after Elizabeth and Jon's arrival to the East Coast, Elizabeth, Jon and Elizabeth's cousin Tony, plus two of Tony's laborers, Juan and Marcos, took on the monumental task of clearing out the first floor rooms of the Hubbard farmhouse in preparation for Tom's memorial reception. The rooms were so full of the scavenging of a pack rat that the furniture and floor were barely visible; they were buried deep beneath an astonishing amount of clutter. The only clearing was a narrow pathway providing access to the center of each room.

There were boxes upon boxes of new and used clothing. There were at least fifteen sets of dishes, coffee cups and glasses, along with plastic bags full of polished and unpolished silverware. Brown paper shopping bags and big green garbage bags brimmed full of sheets, blankets and bedspreads, many with the store tags still attached. There were ten vacuum cleaners, both canisters and uprights. And there were piles upon piles of old newspapers, unopened junk mail, out of date phonebooks and yellowed bank statements. Floor lamps poked out of the mess, their dusty, ornate Victorian lampshades hovered above the mounds like canopies on ornamental trees.

Elizabeth put herself in charge of the cleaning crew. Mrs. Hubbard complained of fatigue and remained upstairs in her bedroom, but Jon and Tony followed Elizabeth from room to room along the narrow pathways. She would open a box, sift through the contents or just point to a pile and Jon and Tony would move it a little bit, into the path or closer to the front door, enough to indicate to Juan or Marcos that it was going out. Then each time the truck that was backed up to the front door became full, much to Tony's displeasure, the junk did *not* go to the dump. To calm his aunt's ragged nerves, he reluctantly agreed to store her multitude of belongings in several units in the U-Store It complex he had built on the land he inherited from his own mother along Route 1.

For the most part, the operation went quickly and smoothly. Except for the few times that Elizabeth lost her patience waiting for Juan and Marcos to return with the truck after taking a load to the storage unit.

"They dodder," Elizabeth would complain to her cousin, who in turn defended the integrity of his two laborers. Yet despite her accusations, by four o'clock in the afternoon, when most of the debris and unnecessary furnishings had been removed, Elizabeth almost thanked the workers. The thought of tipping them had even crossed her mind, but she dismissed it. She told herself that their slow pace was partially to blame for the amount of cleaning that still needed to be done.

Elizabeth felt overwhelmed. The wide-board pine floors needed washing. The flowery wallpaper in the corners of the parlor needed reattaching. The yellowed windowpanes needed cleaning and the curtains washing and pressing. The fireplaces still contained ashes from fires of ten or twenty years earlier. The furniture needed polishing. The cushions and upholstery required vacuuming. The pictures on the walls begged to be straightened. She and Jon had yet to meet with the caterer, the church administrator and the funeral home. Her mother, still hidden upstairs, was useless.

"This is just too much work!" Flabbergasted, Elizabeth turned to her husband, Jon, and asked him to remind her why they had decided against renting a hall.

Juan and Marcos had sensed Elizabeth's dismay and suggested to Tony, who spoke a smattering of Spanish, that Elizabeth hire their entire families to return in the morning and take care of the cleaning. They promised Elizabeth would be satisfied. "Señora Elizabeth será satisfecha," they told Tony. Tony relayed the message to Elizabeth, who, encouraged by her husband, unenthusiastically agreed to allow Juan and Marcos's families to clean the first floor rooms of the farmhouse. "Including the kitchen," Elizabeth stressed.

At 7:30 the following morning, one day before the reception, two vehicles pulled into the circular driveway. Thirteen members of Juan and Marcos's families piled out. Juan's mother, aunt, son, daughter and wife were all there. Marcos's two sisters and their daughters and sons, as well as his mother and grandmother were also prepared to work. Shortly after the families' arrival, Marcos and Juan showed up with one of Tony's work trucks and plenty of cleaning supplies. The two men then led the cleaning crew through the first floor rooms of the house. By the time Elizabeth and Jon had dressed and come down the stairs from their bedroom on the second floor, the first floor was a flurry of activity.

Marcos's grandmother, Gabriella, a dark, round, compassionate yet strong Salvadorian woman, took an immediate interest in Elizabeth and offered with gestures and broken English to make her coffee. Like Elizabeth, she, too, had lost loved ones, she said: two brothers, her father and husband during the civil war in El Salvador. Elizabeth accepted the coffee and, unable to understand a word Gabriella had to say, decided to step out of the way and let them clean, the same way she stepped out of the way when the immigrants cleaned her house in California.

Stirred by all the commotion, Mrs. Hubbard eventually left her bedroom and descended the stairs. On the first floor landing she burst into tears, horrified at what she saw. All of her treasures were gone. Her bounty of boxes of clothing and piles of dishes were gone. Her stacks of newspapers and collections of phone books had been removed. Her brown paper bags and green plastic bags stuffed with bedding still wrapped in plastic were now in storage. All the things she had started to accumulate soon after her husband died, the things she began to amass more deliberately after Tom left town and the things she began to collect at a fevered pace when her daughter Elizabeth moved to the West Coast and married—all of it was simply gone. All that remained in her home were the bare furnishings.

The house was too empty for Mrs. Hubbard. She went into the kitchen and sat at the unusually clean kitchen table, folded her arms into a cradle in front of her, lowered her gray-haired head and wept yet again. Sympathetic, Marcos's youthful mother, Marcia, his soulful grandmother, Gabriella, and Juan's thickset Salvadorian mother, Patella, flocked around Mrs. Hubbard. Cooing and consoling in Spanish—"Pobresita," and "Ahora su hijo esta con Dios"—they made her tea and eggs and toast.

By five o'clock that evening, the two families had transformed the first floor of the Hubbard farmhouse.

They washed the floors, straightened the pictures on the walls, polished the knick-knacks and readied the dining room for the caterer. They organized the kitchen and arranged the furniture in the large living room and parlor to host small gatherings of mourners and to encourage intimate conversations at the memorial reception. Juan's son, Eduardo, cleaned the fireplaces in each room, then drove over to Tony's house and returned with a load of dried wood. In each fireplace he assembled the wood just so—all they needed was a match.

In the fading November light, the rooms glowed with newfound warmth. When Elizabeth and Jon returned from meetings with the priest, the caterer and the undertaker, they were struck by how much the rooms looked like a cozy country inn.

In the small sitting room, between the kitchen and the larger living room, Gabriella and Patella had positioned a stuffed armchair counter-corner to the fireplace. With the addition of a hand-knit afghan blanket, they made the chair as comfortable as possible for Mrs. Hubbard to sit in and receive her guests. On the mantel above the two hundred year old stone fireplace, at Mrs. Hubbard's request, the women placed a small cross, a fat, round white candle and a picture of Tom in his military dress uniform. In the same room, on the small tables on either side of the couch, and on the coffee table, the women set out additional pictures of Tom that Mrs. Hubbard had brought down from her bedroom: Tom as a boy on a bicycle, his high school graduation photo with cap and gown, a college photo with thick sideburns and one of Tom on his 18th birthday, his face tellingly turned away from Mr. Hubbard, who stood beside him. The photo was taken just days before the old man had died.

When they had finished, Juan, Marcos and the

younger members of the crew waited outside while the older women, Gabriella and Patella, slowly walked with Mrs. Hubbard through each room. Together they applied the final touches. In the front parlor, for instance, off the entrance hallway, they made a small adjustment to the position of a photo, in the living room they changed the tilt of a lampshade and in the smaller sitting room they moved a pillow that was ever so slightly out of place—last minute details that made all the difference to a welcoming home. As Gabriella and Patella prepared to leave, Mrs. Hubbard hugged each one and wept with appreciation for their help.

Outside in the driveway, with Marcos translating, Mrs. Hubbard thanked the families and, addressing the older women of the group, said, "Please, all of you, please, come to the reception tomorrow. You must come."

Elizabeth stood in the doorway and rolled her eyes.

Chapter Eleven

After the limousine dropped them off at the front door of the farmhouse, Elizabeth and Jon guided Mrs. Hubbard through a small gathering of mourners and well-wishers from the town. But although the fire in the front parlor was burning and bowls of nuts and chips had been set out, that room was empty of mourners when they passed through. The large living room was also free of guests—except for two. At the far end of the room, in front of the tall window with a circular top, two disheveled old men sat in wooden chairs. They were drinking straight whisky from plastic cups. Jon had never seen them before. Mrs. Hubbard ignored them. And Elizabeth refused to acknowledge them until they spoke.

"Edward wouldn't have liked this," one old man said.

"Nope," the other agreed.

"How nice that you two could make it," Elizabeth said dryly as she and Jon continued to guide her mother into the next room, the reception room, where the chair that had been prepared for her the day before now waited by yet another fire.

"Who were they?" asked Jon when they reached the reception room.

"My brothers-in-law," Mrs. Hubbard spoke as she sat down. "Those two, God love 'em, are so heartless, they would skin a cat alive."

"They're Peter and Alley Hubbard, my father's brothers. They only show up at funerals."

"Oh?"

"They're bigger bastards than my father was."

"Lizzy, not today, please." Mrs. Hubbard settled back into the chair.

"The scum bags tried to take all our land when my father died, saying that when my parents married, my mother's property became my father's, and that it should stay in the family, as in *their* side of the family. Couple of drunks is what they are."

"Lizzy!"

"Well, Mother, you know they are. The jackasses even hired a lawyer, saying my father willed them something that wasn't his to begin with."

"Oh, I remember you telling me all this." Jon began to walk out of the room toward the kitchen.

Elizabeth widened her eyes and looked at him, expecting an explanation.

"I'm only going to check on Arnaldo—the caterer. Let him know that we're here and see if he needs anything."

Jon paused to look at Mrs. Hubbard, now seated in the chair by the fire. She was gazing at the picture of Tom that stood on the mantle. With her stringy gray hair pulled back into a bun and the black shawl wrapped around her hunched shoulders, cheeks sagging sadly with age and a hard life, Jon suddenly felt compassion for his mother-in-law. *She was just a simple farmwoman,* he thought. "Casey, can I bring you anything?"

Mrs. Hubbard thought for a moment. "A whiskey, Jon. Yes, a glass of whiskey would be nice."

"Mother!"

"Lizzy, would you light the candle on the mantle,

please? The one beside your brother."

"I don't know why you need whiskey. You know it doesn't mix with your medication. Plus, you're going to be too hot by this fire. Mother, I think—"

"Lizzy, light the candle," Mrs. Hubbard said, cutting off her daughter.

As Elizabeth lit a match, the sound of people filling the house drifted into the small room. Mrs. Hubbard folded both hands on her lap, ready to receive her guests.

Chapter Twelve

Father Hilliard poked his bald head into the small reception room where Mrs. Hubbard, shawl draped over her shoulders, sat alone, meditatively sipping whiskey from a plastic cup. She seemed lost in thought, watching the cackling fire in the fireplace. Father Hilliard gradually approached, allowing his old eyes time to adjust to the dimly lit room. He peered down at the frail form in the chair. He had known her since first assuming duties at the church over fifty years ago.

"Here you are," he said, gently touching her shoulder.

Glancing up into his soft face, she, too, thought of their decades-long association. "Please, Father, join me." She offered her hand, which he took. "Thank you, Father, you did wonderfully today."

"How are you holding up?"

Her fingers were thinner and colder than he remembered. Her eyes looked foggy. The deep blue pools he had once longed for were now filled with grayness and uncertainty. He had carried this woman through many hardships, guided her through the death of parents, the death of a husband, the death of a brother and sister and now this, the death of her son.

The first time she reached out to him was shortly after his arrival to his new congregation in Newbury. He had responded to her with a sympathetic ear. Her husband was serving in Korea. And although she prayed for her husband's well being, she felt terribly hopeless and full of worry. She had witnessed the effects a war can have on a person. Her own father returned from World War II a changed man. *Would this war do the same to her husband? Would Edward return the same as the man that left? Would war make him calmer, or even more prone to late night explosions of anger?*

Father Hilliard had listened to her concerns. And when she broke down and cried he put an arm around her as any priest might. As he did, he felt the softness of her sweater and smelled the sweetness of her perfume, so he pulled her tighter against him.

She had said, "No." But he persisted.

She tried to push him off. But he forced himself upon her.

Overpowering her, Father Hilliard pinned her to the couch, pushed up her skirt and told her she simply longed for her husband and that he could help. She cried as he climbed on top of her.

"I guess I'm holding up," Mrs. Hubbard said, looking into the fire and then at Tom's photo on the mantel. "Would you sit with me, Father Hilliard?"

He patted her hand in a show of support and then sat in a chair next to the couch.

The next time he raped her, she was still without child. That was ten years later, on a late Saturday afternoon.

She was alone in the function hall in the basement of the church. He was uncertain as to why she was there alone, but he remembered that she had been cleaning the large, electric coffeemaker. He slid up behind her and massaged her neck. Then he slowly began to kiss behind her ear. She struggled to break free, but once again he persisted. As he subdued her, he told her he knew she longed for him. And that through him God could do what her husband couldn't. When she finally stopped struggling, he pushed her back onto one of cold metal tables, took off her slacks and pushed himself deep inside.

"We've been through a lot together, you and I," Father Hilliard reflected, following Mrs. Hubbard's gaze to the photo of Tom.

"Yes," Mrs. Hubbard spoke as if from a distant memory. "You know, he saw you once." She took a sip of whiskey. "In the vestry. He was just a little boy."

"So long ago ... I thought that was all behind us now."

"But I never told him what really happened. Even when he was older." Mrs. Hubbard continued. "Even when he asked me about it. He wanted to know why I had cried and if it hurt. I told him it was nothing. That Mommy had a sore back and Father Hilliard was only helping her to straighten it. I don't know if he believed me or not, but he never asked about it again." She bit on the corner of her lip. "What if this is the Lord's way? What if what happened between us, and now Tom's death, is the Lord's way of—"

Father Hilliard interrupted, "Casey, he was just a boy. I'm sure he believed you."

He paused and asked God for guidance before he spoke again. "Why punish yourself for the past? The Lord is powerful, yes, but forgiving. Our Lord, a loving God, didn't take Tom from you. He called upon Tom for a higher service—a position which Tom was most worthy to accept."

He reached over and placed a hand upon her knee.

"Casey, Tom is now in the service of the Lord."

"I know, Father," she said, glancing toward the fire again. "When Tom was here he used to light fires in these fireplaces. There hasn't been a fire in this house in years."

Chapter Thirteen

Ezekiel, Carrie Phillips and her son, Tommy, pushed their way through the front door and into the crowded entrance hallway of the Hubbard farmhouse. Little Tommy tugged on his mother's arm signaling an accident was eminent. Carrie looked down at her son's round desperate face and tapped Ezekiel's elbow. "Listen," she spoke softly, trying to keep her comments private, "I enjoyed talking with you, and I hope to see you later, but right now I've got to find this little man a bathroom."

"I think I'll be easy to spot in this crowd," Ezekiel said, gesturing toward the white mourners surrounding them. On top of that, he was about a foot taller than almost everyone else.

Carrie and Tommy rushed through the dining room, past the caterer's table and skirted the group that had gathered around the self-serve bar. Ezekiel watched them move, Carrie's head bowed, Tommy pulling her as if they were hurrying through a maze.

Ezekiel surveyed the collection of people in the front parlor. The sadness he had carried for most of the day was now hidden away deep in his chest cavity and a sensation similar to meeting an old friend, something verging on joy, welled in its place. Ezekiel loved crowds. He loved meeting people. And these people especially because he saw them as Tom's people. After years of hearing about and practically knowing them from a distance, he would finally meet his partner's family and small town friends in person.

Ezekiel moved through the parlor; the small room was crowded and the flames from the lit fireplace made it hot as a furnace. *Who are these people?* he wondered. *Distant cousins? High school friends? College? Sports? Teacher? Family doctor? Dentist?*

A bulky, tall man, yet still shorter than Ezekiel, stood in the doorway between the parlor and the living room. Sharply attired in a gray business suit, he nodded a greeting.

"Hi, I'm Neil Bingham." Feeling slightly intimidated by Ezekiel, Neil felt the need to validate his presence: "An old high school friend of Tom's."

Ezekiel leaned forward and took Neil's extended hand. "Pleased to meet you, Neil. My name is Ezekiel. I was close to Tom in Arlington ... Virginia," he clarified.

Neil Bingham from high school? Tom had shared numerous stories about his school days—mostly related to athletics, namely track. His favorite ones he'd recap during their pillow talk at night, sort of romantic versions of the 'high jinks' of small town teenagers. Tom had repeated the same stories enough times, however, that Ezekiel, a city boy, treasured the tales and could recite them as if they were his own. *But Neil Bingham?* he puzzled. The name sounded familiar, yet he had trouble placing it.

"I knew him from high school," Neil repeated. "Sad."

"Terrible."

"Long drive up from ... Virginia?"

"I flew."

"Me, too, from Chicago."

"Chicago?"

"Couldn't believe it when I heard. What did you say? You worked with Tom?"

"No," Ezekiel nervously laughed. Since arriving in the area, this was Ezekiel's first conversation that involved Tom's death. And thus the first in which he would need to keep their relationship a secret. On the plane ride up, he had thought these conversations would be best handled by picturing Tom alive at home, in their house, waiting for him to return. That way he wouldn't have to deal with his loss while simultaneously trying to conceal their relationship. He knew Newbury was not Arlington, and that these people were not like their friends back home. Those people, his and Tom's friends, had all gathered around Ezekiel and supported him. They tended to his emotional needs; he cried on many shoulders. There, at home in Arlington, Tom's death and their relationship were very real and he could mourn openly. But up here, in Tom's hometown, he was on his own, alone with his emotions. "Work together? No, no. We were just very close."

"Oh, neighbors?"

"You might say that."

Although Ezekiel had accepted Tom's decision, he hated it. He hated when he encountered Tom's "barriers to freedom." But out of respect for his partner, Ezekiel moved the conversation away from his relationship with Tom. "Well, you two must go way back then ... high school. Wow. When was the last time you saw him?"

"Just talking about that this morning. Five years ago Christmas, I think. But yeah, I'd say he was one of my best friends. It was me, that thin guy over there ..." Neil raised an arm over people's heads and pointed across the room, "Ted Dorsey, and another guy, Julian Reynolds, who didn't make it, or at least I haven't seen him yet ... and some of his cousins. You know, the old high school gang. But things change, you know. I can't believe how things are so different around here, the new houses and all. Yeah, so I figure it had to be five years anyway, since I'd seen him last."

"Ted Dorsey?" Ezekiel said aloud, familiar with that name. Ted and his wife, Shelly, were two of the people he had hoped to meet.

"You know him?" Neil asked, surprised.

"Oh no, but the name sounds familiar. Maybe Tom mentioned it or something—"

From the corner of his eye, through the crowd, Ezekiel saw a short, stout man with hefty arms and big hands coming toward them, a well-manicured woman following behind.

"Bing!" the man said excitedly. "The Binger! The Binger is back in town. I heard you were here. Look at that belly. Looks like someone's packing it on!"

"Jesus Christ, Billy Quinn! Hey, I wouldn't go bragging, if I were you," Neil said, patting his own stomach and pointing to Billy's at the same time.

Ezekiel recognized Neil's nickname and put it together—*So this is Bing, the big sports ego of the gang.* He took a step back and allowed the woman to join the group.

"Bing, you ever meet my wife, Jeannine? You might remember her from high school? She used to be an Olson." They shook hands. No motion was made to introduce Ezekiel. "So whatcha up to these days, bro? Where you living now? Haven't seen you in years."

Ezekiel listened to the exchange about what their lives had become since they had last seen each other. No kids; three kids. Not married, but still looking; married eleven years. Into marketing; contractor. Two straight men jockeying for each others' respect after years of no contact, accompanied by a woman with bright red lipstick and a gold crucifix around her neck. She even smiled and giggled on cue. They mystified Ezekiel. And they ignored him. Eventually, however, his presence became obvious. His bright, forced smile alone was enough to intimidate them into acknowledging him.

"So, who's your friend?" Billy Quinn asked.

"I'm sorry, shit, we just met here."

"Oh," Billy and his wife, Jeannine, sized up Ezekiel and stopped short of offering their hands.

"Sorry, I forgot your name," Neil said sheepishly.

"Ezekiel."

"Ezekiel. That's quite a name. This here's my wife, Jeannine, and I'm Billy Quinn. Tom is, uh, was, my cousin."

"Nice to meet you both. And I'm sorry you lost your cousin," Ezekiel said, although he had the impression that none of them cared what he said.

"Shit, Bing, I noticed you and him talking and I thought you found yourself a new knob-polisher," Billy joked, snorting out a half-laugh.

Jeannine shrank in embarrassment.

Neil shoved Billy and they both laughed. "You're not still onto that, are you? I can't believe you remember that."

Ezekiel stepped back from the circle.

"Just an old joke," Billy explained. "Goes back to high school when we were both on the swim team. There was always this one big dumb guy we picked on. We called him the knob-polisher, because he was big but kind of, well, kinda dainty. He was like our team mascot, if you know what I mean." Billy leaned forward and spoke as though he were letting Ezekiel in on a secret: "Sort of a big, fairy towel-boy." He straightened up, like he had just suitably explained himself.

"Shut up," Jeannine said under her breath as she lightly punched Billy in the side.

"Let's see, what was that kid's name? I swear—" Billy rubbed his chin and quizzically looked at Neil for help.

Neil's eyes were on Ezekiel, however.

Billy quickly changed his demeanor when he realized that the big black man, twice his size, wasn't laughing. "Hey, man, I was only kidding. You know, just an old high school joke. I hope I didn't offend."

Ezekiel extended his large hand for Billy Quinn to shake. Billy, relieved, responded in kind. Ezekiel wrapped his fingers firmly around Billy's hand. "I trust you don't pass this type of humor onto your kids?"

Without loosening his grip, Ezekiel held Billy's gaze and stared down into his eyes. Billy Quinn swallowed hard and Ezekiel felt he had finally caught a glimpse of what Tom's youthful struggle must have been like, the things Tom never mentioned about growing up in Newbury. He thought, *Sometimes fighting's not worth it. It's easier to leave it alone—keep quiet, leave town, move away—like Tom did.*

"I'm really just here to pay my respects to Tom's family," Ezekiel said. "But I've enjoyed making your acquaintance."

He let go of Billy's hand and, tipping his head, extended his 'best wishes' toward Jeannine, excused himself from Neil and moved further into the living room in search of more enlightening conversations.

Chapter Fourteen

Melanie parked in the cul-de-sac at the end of the new road behind the Hubbard farmhouse and, with an air of entitlement, walked across the close-trimmed grass that spread around the grounds of the new neighborhood. She followed the old path through the haying fields of her childhood. Although covered over by sod, the route was hard-wired into her. Generations of her family had moved across the fields, by foot, horse and wagon and, more recently, by tractor. Without a second thought, she cut between two oversized colonial houses, walking across the green swaths that served as backyards and past two identical children's play sets and second floor decks that looked out toward the Hubbard house. Then, effortlessly, she hopped over a post and rail fence and stepped over the stonewall that separated the neighborhood from the remnants of the old Quinn farm.

On the Hubbard side of the property, from the stonewall all the way to the Hubbard's kitchen door, the path remained unaltered. Tall, tough grass lined the path which twisted past discarded cooking pots riddled with shotgun pellet holes, old broken milk crates and the smiling, slumbering, rusted chassis of a 1957 Ford pickup truck. Bits of rope still hung from the grayed wooden poles of the abandoned clothesline.

The back door of the house was unlocked. The rear entryway had escaped the previous day's cleaning. To pass through to the kitchen, Melanie had to move out of the way old broom handles, dried mop heads, several galvanized buckets and an old apple bushel basket filled with paper bags. She managed to open the door just enough to pass into the kitchen. Nobody looked familiar, so she stood by the door, brushed off the front of her brown sweater and tugged her jacket's lapel. She pushed her black hair behind an ear, but several strands immediately returned to thier natural position against her cheek. Conversations filled the kitchen—"Will the rain ever let up?" "The service was beautiful," and "I agree with the President's strategy. I think we're winning the war."

A loud, clanging noise broke the mourners' chatter. The caterer's assistant had dropped a stack of silver tray lids as he tried to push past people and return to the dining room through the kitchen access hallway. The lids scattered across the kitchen floor, forcing the mourners to momentarily stop their conversations and switch positions. Other guests, those who had waited at the front of the food line in the dining room, entered the kitchen carrying plastic plates with small servings of rice, chicken and vegetables. They surrounded the assistant caterer as he tried his best to quickly stack the lids and get out of the way.

To Melanie, the scene looked more like a party than a reception for a dead soldier. She immediately wanted to leave. *Be sociable, be sociable,* she coached herself. *No, just see if he's here, then find my aunt, pay my respects and leave. That's it.* Her face reddened as embarrassment at being alone took hold. *Had she stood by the back door for too long? What if people noticed?* She had to move—

But where?

The door to the small sitting room was closed and guests holding plates clogged the access hall to the dining room. *Shit.* Melanie began to panic. *Christ, when did I become so fucking frightened? I hate this!* To protect herself, to keep others from noticing her angst, she faked a smile in the direction of a tall, blonde woman who turned her head away without smiling back.

"Well, look who decided to show up," Elizabeth called out, pushing through the crowd. "It's about time. She keeps asking for you."

Heads turned in Melanie's direction. She wanted to slink away.

Approaching her cousin, Elizabeth continued speaking: "Mel, I didn't see you come in. I've been hanging around the front door trying to greet people. I left Jon up there. Can you believe it? Look at this place."

"Crowded."

"No shit! That old pervert priest told the papers the times for the funeral and burial, even though I asked him not to. You should have been there this morning at the burial. It was mobbed. Then that old jackass made an announcement inviting everybody here. Not only that—" Elizabeth lowered her voice, "but my mother pretty much gave him the go ahead to do it."

"Wow."

"No shit."

Ever since Elizabeth had moved to California after high school, and then married Jon seven years ago, her relationship with Melanie, not that it had ever been brilliant, deteriorated to Christmas and birthday cards. Melanie had met Jon only once before and she had never met their children. But then again, Elizabeth had never invited Melanie to visit them in California.

"You look good, Mel," Elizabeth complimented her

cousin with the tone of a patronizing mother praising a child for having cleaned her bedroom.

"Thanks, Liz." Melanie had difficulty looking her cousin in the eye. Jealous, Elizabeth had done all the things that Melanie had dreamed of as a little girl— moving to California, marrying a loving husband, having children.

"I hear the kids didn't come. But Jon's with you; must be a big help."

"He's certainly done his part for the family. He helped me to organize the caterer, clean the house, everything. The house turned out amazing. Have you seen it?" Almost without thinking, Elizabeth touched Melanie's arm, but Melanie pulled it back close to her chest. Elizabeth continued, undaunted: "Tony helped me some, too. Anyway we got the place into ship-shape. She'd become such a packrat. I am sure you know. Really, you have to take a look around."

"Yeah, Tony told me. I hadn't been over in awhile," Melanie said, checking the front of her sweater again. Her cousin's firm body, sexy black dress, perfect makeup and straight, jet-black hair only heightened her jealousy. And on top of that, Melanie felt sure Elizabeth was putting her down for her inattentiveness to her aunt's needs. But she knew from Tony that Elizabeth and Jon had actually hired people to transform the house. *Once again*, Melanie reflected, *just like when we were kids— Elizabeth, always the center of attention, taking credit for everything.*

"How's Aunt Casey holding up?"

"Surprisingly well. She's in there."

Elizabeth pointed to the small room and leaned closer to Melanie. "I think she likes the attention. She's been lonely, you know, and this brings people to her. In a funny way, I think it's good for her."

Melanie pulled back. Elizabeth's face, so close to her own, made her uncomfortable. But Elizabeth persevered, and, leaning further in, continued to explain how she had arranged everything. "And because it was so damp and cold, I insisted that the limo drive us from the cemetery to here. Then we set up a comfortable spot for Mother by the fire to receive guests. And Jon and I have been monitoring the number of people who can sit with her at any one time. You know, we're trying to move people through."

"You're in charge," Melanie said, stepping awkwardly away from her cousin and reluctantly toward the crowd in the center of the kitchen.

Chapter Fifteen

Julian took the back roads. He thought it best. Because after drinking close to a pint of vodka, not only did his stomach threaten upheaval but the muscles in his arms twitched and pulled unpredictably. He would have drunk more to relax those symptoms, making it easier to drive, but he had finished the bottle and there was nothing left to drink in the apartment. So instead of blasting his beat-up car down Interstate 495 at 80 miles an hour on the outside chance that he could still make the tail end of Tom's burial ceremony, he slowly maneuvered the back roads like a pokey old man.

He thought of stopping to pick up a fresh bottle of vodka. He would need one to make it through the day. And although he would pass two liquor stores on the way to Newbury and the Hubbard farmhouse, he had had prior bad experiences with each. At the first store, the owner once refused to sell him a pint of vodka and then threatened to call the cops when he stumbled drunkenly back to his car. At the second store, a police cruiser was usually parked adjacent to the front of the building—sort of a permanent, small town speed trap. They had pulled him over twice after leaving that store, and twice, as fortune would have it, they let him go. So Julian passed by the first store. And, afraid his good luck on this road would run out, he straightened his driving posture until he was safely past the second one, too.

It was after two in the afternoon by the time he got to Newbury. He drove past the quiet white church on High Road where the funeral had taken place. Though he realized he had missed the burial ceremony, still, he considered it his duty to go to the gravesite and pay respects to a dead friend. After that, he figured a short drive across town to the memorial reception at the Hubbard farmhouse. Melanie had said it would likely run all afternoon. *So it'll be the gravesite, then the reception. But first things first.* He swung a right off of High Road and headed toward the ever-faithful, Charlie's Package Store for a bottle.

Chapter Sixteen

"Shell, pack up the kids and come on over. Tom's reception has turned out to be an open house, kind of a party," Ted Dorsey told his wife.

"Should we?" Shelly could hear the crowd through the telephone receiver.

"Yeah, it's like everyone's here. The Quinn's kids are here."

"But they're family."

"That doesn't matter. Besides, I think Mrs. Hubbard would love to see 'em."

Shelly agreed to go, but in truth she was reluctant to stop what she was doing, ready their two children, pack them into their car seats and drive across town. After her father had reneged on a promise to baby-sit, and after Ted left to pick up Neil Bingham, she spent the morning cleaning house. Not that the house was dirty or disorganized or even needed the thorough attention she gave it, but she was angry—mad at her father for backing out, jealous that Ted got to go to the funeral, the gravesite and the memorial reception while she was, once again, stuck at home with the children. But more than the anger toward her father, more than the jealousy of Ted, she felt as if staying home and cleaning were penitence to God for having been secretly and selfishly excited about attending all the affairs of the day.

When she thought about it, it was obvious: She had let excitement and anticipation about spending a day out amongst adults override the tragedy behind the circumstances. The previous evening, for example, after putting the children to bed, she weeded through the fancier clothes in the back of the closet—clothing stored in long, clear plastic bags since before her second pregnancy. Some outfits she'd almost forgotten she owned.

Standing in front of the dresser mirror she tried on smart dresses, sophisticated skirts and tasteful blouses. At first she limited the choices to dark colors, but soon she was putting on a personal fashion show, like a child playing dress up. At one point, she even practiced mock adult conversations about politics, careers, books and restaurants. She pictured herself dining in London, New York and Paris—"Reservations for Dorsey?" "Two, please, yes." "Why, thank you. You are so kind."

Although Shelly had never traveled to London, New York and Paris, and figured she never would, still, she missed the freedom that she and Ted had enjoyed before marriage and before the birth of their children had refined her dreams. And for a moment she fancied herself living a different life—a life like she had always imagined Tom Hubbard had led. In the end, however, she decided on a conservative but definitely stylish, dark green, close-to-black blazer, black slacks and a matching sweater. The lack of color would complement Ted's suit. Her fashion assessment: "Respectful of Tom, and perfect for a damp November day." Then she laid the ensemble over the back of their bedroom chair.

Later that evening, after choosing her outfit, Shelly knelt at the foot of their bed and folded her hands to pray.

"God, please bless my family and Tom's heroic soul. God, of course I'm grateful for all that I have ... my children and my husband, our family. But, God, so few things change in my life, so little happens. And I know this is wrong ... I'm ashamed of myself for feeling this ... But—I am all jumpy and excited, like I'm going to a wedding, or like something special will happen tomorrow. Bless my family. Bless Tom's soul. And please, God, forgive me for my selfishness."

The following morning the phone rang while the two children were arguing over toast and soft-boiled eggs. Her husband, dressed in his suit, paced the kitchen floor, aimlessly grumbling about his 'hyperactive sense of responsibility'—not only had he offered to pick Neil Bingham up at the airport, a fifty minute ride each way, but he had promised to drive him back as well, that same night, so Neil could catch a return flight to Chicago. Before even answering the phone, Shelly correctly guessed it was her father calling to cancel. She knew she'd have to stay home because, *God is always watching us.*

"Thanks, Dad," was all she said. Then she commenced with a thorough cleaning of the house.

Now, moments after hanging up with her husband, who had not only said to come to the memorial reception but to bring the kids as well, Shelly thought aloud, "I guess I've paid the price and learned my lesson: Today is Tom's day, not my day. Thank you, God, for helping me see that."

Shelly was unaware that her son, five-year-old Teddy, had heard her speaking out loud.

"Are we going out?" Teddy looked up at her with inquisitive brown eyes. After dressing the children in their best play clothes, clean jeans and a blue button down shirt for pudgy Teddy and an attractive pink jumpsuit for her bubbly four-year-old Tammy, Shelly changed her own clothes. For herself, she decided on a different outfit, one more fitting for the occasion than the one laid out the night before—this time it was a pair of simple slacks and a plain blouse. *Definitely less flashy*, she thought. She got Teddy and Tammy into the family car and arrived at the Hubbard farmhouse just a few short minutes later.

Chapter Seventeen

Jon Goldberg hardly ever drank alcohol. However, the gray, raw November day, accented by the dancing flames in the fireplaces of the Hubbard farmhouse and the multitude of smartly dressed folks conversing around them, created a romantic New England atmosphere that called for a glass. Or maybe it was just the way the big black man in the living room comfortably held his plastic cup of red wine that made the idea of having one seem so appealing. Either way, Jon abandoned his post as official greeter, a position his commanding wife, Elizabeth, had assigned him, and went to join the crowd at the makeshift bar in the dining room.

Arnaldo the caterer looked up from the serving line and waved to Jon entering the room. Jon replied with a close-mouthed smile that turned his full red lips into thin pink lines. He raised his thick, black eyebrows into an expression he thought coy and cool—understated, but clearly issuing a friendly hello. Unfortunately, Jon's signature greeting had the same effect on Arnaldo as it did on the paralegals at the office, his law partners and all who visited the firm: It hid any warmth and left others feeling as though he were snobby, disinterested, or, worse, dissatisfied with them. Arnaldo, now convinced

Jon was unhappy with his work, turned his attention back to the serving line, feeling a little more disgruntled with his employers for underestimating the size of the party. Jon felt satisfied though, and, thinking of Arnaldo as a friend, turned away and proceeded to the bar.

Once there, Jon was surprised to find that some guests must have brought their own beverages. The selection he and Elizabeth had approved with Arnaldo, a case each of red and white wine, two cases of imported beer and some of the harder liquors—whisky, scotch, vodka and gin—was dwarfed by what now looked like an abundantly stocked bar. There were eight open bottles of different red wines.

Jon didn't know one from the other. He pursed his lips and pushed up his cheeks as if a connoisseur scrutinizing the possibilities that hid behind the labels. Wondering if he and Elizabeth even owned a bottle of wine, Jon determined that in fact they did; they had had a party last year and after it ended he had moved a box with several leftover bottles out to the garage.

But the last time he had actually had a glass of wine, he recalled, was on the Jewish New Year, when he, Elizabeth and the children had been invited to their friends the Levine's for dinner. Jon's mother, on the other hand, was known to take the occasional drink and even become a little tipsy. Not Jon. As an undergraduate he got drunk several times, but by senior year he was finished with that.

Jon was lost in thought when the man next to him spoke: "You gonna have to pick one of 'em." Two scrawny, dirty-looking, older men had sneaked up next to him; Elizabeth's two uncles, Peter and Ally Hubbard, were picking up bottles by their necks and placing them back down in their search for the whiskey.

"The way you looking at that bottle there, you must

be an aficionado," said the other brother, his speech lagging from the drinking he had begun hours earlier.

"Me?" Jon smiled his signature thin smile and raised his eyebrows. He noticed pieces of chicken in Alley Hubbard's bushy, gray mustache. "Actually, I don't know one from the other."

"Let me introduce myself then," Peter Hubbard said. "I'm Julio Gallo and this here's my brother, Ernest Gallo." The two men started laughing.

"Pleased to meet you," Jon said, trying to hide the fact that their sarcasm had insulted him. He remembered their proper names from when Elizabeth had briefly recapped their contentious history with the family. So choosing not to carry the exchange any further and he turned back to the drawing of a vineyard on the label of the bottle in his hand.

"Found it!" said Alley Hubbard, twisting the brown screw top off a liter of whisky.

"Top 'em off!" ordered Peter Hubbard, pushing a plastic cup to the space on the table between the two of them.

Alley wiped his mustache, poured whisky into the plastic cups and leaned forward over the bar to see around his brother.

"We seen you come in with Lizzy. You her husband?" He pointed at Jon with the neck of the bottle he held.

"He'd best be," laughed Peter Hubbard as he picked up a plastic cup and turned to face Jon.

"Yes, I am. We've been married seven years now." Jon adopted what he thought was a pleasant tone.

"We're Lizzy's uncles, her father's brothers," said Alley Hubbard.

"Well, nice to meet you."

"Is that so? You hear that, Alley?" Peter Hubbard put

a boney hand on Alley's fragile looking shoulder. "The man here says it's nice to meet you. I bet it is."

"He marries our niece," Alley Hubbard ran his fingers through his mustache again and chicken crumpled out, "our brother's only daughter, and he don't even invite us to the Goddamn wedding." Alley Hubbard cocked his head to the side. "Nice to meet you, you say?"

"This one here," Peter Hubbard spoke loudly with a drunken slur and turning to the other guests in the dining room, "this one here, he drags our family off to California, marries our brother's daughter, then comes back and says, 'Nice to meet you.'" Extending an arm toward the center of the room, Peter Hubbard scrunched up his face and spit out, "We hears you have kids and don't go so far ... won't even lift a finger or nothin' ... as to tell us nothin' about 'em."

"Well, I ..."

"Well, nothin'," Alley Hubbard pointed directly at Jon. "You come back here, now that Tom's dead, acting like you own the Goddamn place. Trying to step into our nephew's rightful shoes."

"What? Wait—" Jon tried to remain calm.

Alley Hubbard's accusation was absurd. If the choice had been his, Jon would have stayed in Los Angles. He had hardly known his brother-in-law Tom, never mind harboring a desire to step into his shoes, whatever that meant. As far as he knew, Tom had washed his hands of this family a long time ago. If, as Jon assumed, these two old men's anger was about Tom's piece of land at the end of the street, then they should pick a fight with someone else, because he had nothing to do with it and wanted nothing to do with it.

"'Wait!'" Peter Hubbard snarled. "'Wait,' he says! We been waitin' fah years! Tells us to wait, and he's back here from California to capitalize on Tom's death! Just 'cause Tom don't got no kids to leave it to, don't mean it's yours, hotshot. Just like that mother-in-law of yours who capitalized on our brother's death. That last piece of land is rightfully ours!"

The mourners in the dining room stood frozen. Arnaldo the caterer stopped serving and came out from behind the row of silver pans; judging by the brothers' snarling expressions and the look of bewilderment on his employer's face, he prepared to break up a fistfight. A little blonde-haired boy who had been playing nearby buried his head in his mother's skirt and began to cry. The concerned mother rushed him into the kitchen access hallway.

"Hold on," Jon said, shaken. As a lawyer he had argued with the most unreasonable of people and won, but senseless, boiling anger intimidated him.

"Hold on, nothing. I'll show you hold on!" Peter Hubbard slammed a cup full of whiskey onto the makeshift bar. The plastic cup's bottom cracked open and in the stillness that followed the only sound heard was the steady drip of whisky forming a puddle on the wide, Pumpkin-Pine floor board.

Jon stepped back. A bead of sweat formed above his brow. Returning the bottle of red wine to the bar, he prepared for—he didn't know what.

Then Elizabeth's cousin, Tony, a man more muscular than both Jon and the Hubbard brothers put together, barged in. Tony pushed his way from the front hallway through the crowd of tense mourners in the dining room, stepping between the three men.

"Easy does it, cowboys," he said in a calm, humorous voice.

Peter and Alley Hubbard were his Aunt Casey's in-laws, related to him through marriage. Like bored dogs that barked, he knew they were harmless; he had dealt with them throughout his life.

Peter Hubbard snidely responded, "Don't you 'boy' us, you little—"

The brothers took off their jackets and rolled up their shirtsleeves, fast shifting their attention from Jon to Tony. They adopted fighting stances that in their youth had probably appeared rather dangerous, but as older men they looked more like worn out farmers who had misplaced their shotguns, refugees from the dust bowl.

"This isn't a barroom, you yahoos. Back off!" Tony had intended to be respectful of the men, but the sight of the two old Hubbard brothers, jackets off, shirtsleeves rolled up, faces ruddy, was too much and he laughed out loud.

"Tell *him* to watch it," Peter Hubbard addressed Tony, pointing to Jon. Then, as fast as it had started, the brothers abandoned their stances, picked up their jackets and cocked their shoulders back like roosters that had battled over a hen and won. Peter Hubbard took a new plastic cup, poured whisky into it and reiterated his threat to Jon: "You best watch your step, city boy."

The two men drunkenly sauntered as best they could across the dining room and into the entrance hallway.

Arnaldo the caterer, happy to have gotten out of playing the role of peacemaker, asked, "Who's next?"

The buffet line re-formed and he began to serve again.

Tony turned to Jon and, adopting a playful tone, asked, "You don't seem like the fighting sort. Why are you picking a fight with those two?"

"I was just—"

"They're harmless pains-in-the-ass anyway. You okay?" Tony asked.

Just then Tony's sister, Melanie, came up behind

and, sliding an index finger through his back belt loop, tugged to get his attention.

"Hey, you made it. About time," he said.

"Hi Jon," Melanie said. The thought of hugging flashed through Jon and Melanie's minds, but they had only met once before, at Jon and Elizabeth's wedding, and so they were practically strangers. Neither made a move.

"You two the ones scaring the little kids? It's like a crying fest in the kitchen," Melanie joked.

"I don't think I could scare a child," Jon replied and offered Melanie his signature smile, relieved the drama had passed. Picking up a bottle of red wine, he pushed out a deep breath and placed the bottle back down. Having a glass of red wine had lost its appeal.

Chapter Eighteen

Carrie Phillips tried to coax her son's tears into remission, but they kept flowing—albeit only for a short time. Her offerings of hugs, chocolates and cookies helped some, but they were no match for all the attention he had begun to receive from a kitchen full of admirers.

The boy was beautifully cute. His eyes had puffed up like sugarcoated pastries and his face had swollen round like a ripe, juicy-red tomato with a stem of golden hair on top. All of his needs were being met—his mother's presence, cookies and a room full of admirers. And with the sudden addition of the Dorsey children, just as quickly as they had started, the tears dried up—he now appeared on the verge of laughter.

Earlier, when Tommy's tears had first started flowing, Teddy and Tammy Dorsey were on the couch in the airless reception room tying their fingers into knots while their mother and father offered formal condolences to Mrs. Hubbard. The sight of the aged woman had frightened the two children. To them she appeared creepy; hunched in a chair with a black shawl draped over her shoulders, she resembled a decrepit Angel of Death—complete with the fires of hell glowing in the fireplace behind her, just like they heard described at Sunday School.

Tammy, the younger of the two, was already close to tears upon hearing Tommy's initial howls coming from the room next door. She looked to her older brother Teddy for help. He tried to remain strong, but the facade rapidly faded when he, too, heard another child's tears. Propelled by a combination of fear of Mrs. Hubbard and a curiosity about the crying emanating from the next room, the Dorsey children jumped off the couch together and rushed into the kitchen. Once there, Tommy's crying proved to be contagious. Within seconds their immunity diminished and the Dorsey children broke into tears, too.

When the gangly Ted Dorsey appeared in the kitchen doorway to check on what trouble his children could have caused, he found Carrie Phillips squatting between the three blubbering children holding a plate of cookies.

"These two are mine. What did they do?" he asked.

"Nothing. I think mine inspired them." Carrie Phillips spoke as she stood and placed a hand on Tommy's head.

With the addition of the Dorsey children, Tommy's admirers had turned away: One tearful blonde boy was cute. Three wailing children in a kitchen full of adults were annoying. Sensing he was no longer the center of attention, Tommy stopped crying.

Carrie brushed her son's hair. "It's been a long day. And then these men started arguing by the bar. It scared the heck out of him."

"I think this whole thing's been hard on these two as well," Ted said, rubbing his children's backs as they wiped their eyes. "We were good friends with Tom," Ted blurted out awkwardly. He'd always been uncomfortable around women he did not know.

When he hesitatingly introduced himself, he noticed the little blonde boy look up as if he had been addressed. "Hello there," Ted said to the boy.

Carrie pulled Tommy close. "Every time he hears the name Tom, he thinks someone's talking to him. His name is Thomas, Tommy, too. I'm Carrie," she said, shaking Ted's hand.

"I'm Ted."

Hardly a conversationalist, he wondered what to say next. But he decided that, although he didn't know her, he liked this woman. Something about her seemed familiar, like someone he had known for years. He tried to relax. "Did you know Tom from Arlington?"

"Arlington, you mean Virginia? No, Tom and me, we first met ten or so years ago. I was really—well, I was shocked when I heard, or, that is, when I saw his name and picture on the news. I didn't even know he was over there—I was just shocked."

"My wife Shelly and I were, too. We were all high school friends."

Ted hesitated again. Speaking of Tom's death made him uneasy. In fact, the whole notion of someone his age dying was new. Other people in his life had died, aunts and uncles, but they were older and their deaths seemed appropriate. Even as a boy, he knew they were going to die; it was inevitable. They were only doing what they were supposed to do. A contemporary's death, however, struck differently. This feeling that Tom existed somewhere in the past, and now that past was permanently gone, taxed Ted's imagination. He struggled with the meaning behind his sadness—was he sad for the end of his past or for Tom's death? Likely both.

Carrie noticed a change in Ted's demeanor. He looked as confused as his son who had just finished crying. "You knew him well then?" she asked.

"He was an usher at our wedding. He called us before he went back over. So, you know, we kept in touch. Where did you know him from?"

"Just around, really—Boston. Then I bumped into him again, and, well, we became friendly. But I haven't seen him in years."

When she had left Boston that morning, Carrie's goal was to introduce her son to his grandmother, but to keep their identities a secret so as to not call attention away from the day's events. She had accomplished that goal at the gravesite. However, after the priest made an announcement inviting everyone to the Hubbard house, she realized she wanted more, not just for herself but also for her son. She wanted Tommy to have more of a memory of his father, something other than just a burial, so that when the boy was older and asked to know more about his father, she could explain it to him through the memory of this day.

"You saw him recently in Boston?" Ted was only half listening to Carrie. His own sadness and confusion weighed on him. Additionally, he was trying to keep an eye on his children. The two had bonded with this woman's son and they were now confidently following the boy through the maze of adults in the kitchen. Typically, his children were shy around older people. He noticed, however, that little Tommy was not.

"No, not recently." She hesitated, and then added, "It would have to be almost five years ago anyway. That was the last time I saw him."

Carrie watched her son move about the kitchen. He would join a group of adults, stand there and look up at them until they looked down at him, and then, as if approving them, he would smile and move on to the next group.

"He's a pretty friendly boy," Ted remarked.

"His father could be, too." Tommy reminded Carrie of his father. Tom Hubbard had had that same confidence. Completely at ease in a crowd, he could talk to anyone.

She had fallen in love with Tom Hubbard almost immediately. She was an undergraduate, a junior at Simmons College, and Tom appeared ideal—older, tall, blonde. And when he looked at her, she melted. They went out only twice. Then he disappeared. Although she dated many other men after Tom, they never measured up to him.

"Yes, he gets his extrovert character from his father."

About six years ago they bumped into each other again in Harvard Square. He invited her for a cappuccino, apologized for disappearing and magically re-entered her life. He would come to Boston and stay for two, three days at a time, then leave. She never asked him why or where he went, but she lived for their time together.

Then she became pregnant. He demanded she get an abortion. She refused. By the time little Tommy was born, Tom had stopped visiting. Every once in a while she would contact him, but it was always a disaster. The last time they talked he called her a whore and said the boy belonged to someone else.

"Did he come today, his father?" Ted asked.

Carrie looked down at the plate of cookies she held. Leaving Ted's question unanswered, she stepped to the closest counter and placed the plate down, returning to Ted's side in time for Shelly Dorsey, Ted's wife, to join them.

"She seems to be holding up. Such a strong woman," Shelly said, referring to Mrs. Hubbard, and then, turning to Carrie, "Hi, I'm Shelly."

A tinge of jealousy clicked in the back of Shelly's mind, comparing her ridged body to Carrie's softer cuteness. She glanced at her husband.

Ted swallowed guiltily: "Shell, this is ... I'm sorry?"

"Carrie."

"She came up from Boston," Ted added.

"Boston! Gosh, Tom got around. I was just commenting to Mrs. Hubbard that it's amazing how many people are here. His life touched so many. Wouldn't you agree?" Shelly asked Carrie.

"Yes," Carrie answered. "I was surprised when we got to the cemetery."

"Ted got to go. I stayed home with our children." Shelly pointed to the boy and girl who were still tagging along behind Tommy as he continued to inspect the adults in the kitchen. "I'm so sorry I missed it. Tom was such a wonderful man. Did your husband know Tom well?"

"My husband?"

"Oh ... I'm sorry. You said 'we,' so I just assumed—" Shelly apologized, embarrassed. She wanted so much for people to think of her as astute, as something more than just a stay-at-home mom. But her stated assumption that Carrie was married and that it was her husband who was connected to Tom only proved how unworldly she was.

"My son and I went to the gravesite," Carrie pointedly responded. Since Tommy's birth, she had considered herself an independent woman, working full-time and taking full responsibility for raising her child. "I'm a single mom," Carrie said, motioning to Tommy.

"That one? ... He's adooorable."

"A little social butterfly," Ted added.

"Thank you," Carrie said. "He can be a handful at times, but he's the love of my life."

"Aren't they all?" Shelly leaned forward, and, much

to Carrie's displeasure, put her hands on her knees and called for Tommy's attention as if calling a dog.

The boy ignored her.

"My, but isn't he a little young to be going to a gravesite?"

Shelly inherently questioned the judgment of all single mothers: If they had done things differently in the first place, they wouldn't be in the jam they were in now. "It must have been a traumatic experience for him?"

"Not at all," Carrie answered. "I thought it was important for him to—" she stopped, realizing that she wanted to explain who her son was and why they were there.

Earlier in the day, when the priest had announced the reception and she decided to attend, her motivation had been unclear. She had simply wanted to give Tommy a fuller picture of his father, a memory to hold on to. But now, speaking to the Dorseys, she understood for the first time what she really wanted—someone else, someone from Tom's life, to know that Tommy was Tom's child. And she wanted to explain to someone, Tom's mother perhaps, how Tom's life, and his absence since her son's birth, had shaped their lives. But these were not the people to share this information with.

"Well, I had two reasons for bringing him." Carrie spoke like the junior high school teacher she was. "First, to share with him my own sadness, and second, to teach him a lesson about war's consequences."

Chapter Nineteen

Over seven years had passed since Father Hilliard had had the opportunity to place a log upon a fire. The fireplace in the rectory living room, where he occasionally entertained parishioners, was now a cleaner, safer, propane-fueled fire. At first he thought the fire looked fake; ceramic logs lit by a fancy gas cooking range. But he soon adapted to the ease and comfort of the gas without the mess of the wood. Besides, guests would all comment that it was impossible for them to tell the difference.

He clapped once and slowly stood, his tired body complaining as he rose. "There, that should do it," he said proudly. Despite the new gas fireplace at the rectory, Father Hilliard had retained that unique piece of knowledge of how to successfully lay logs upon a fire.

"Perfect," Mrs. Hubbard said to him.

"Bien," Marco's grandmother, Gabriella, and Juan's mother, Patella, who the day before had helped clean the house and ready the sitting room for Mrs. Hubbard, agreed in unison from their position on the couch. The older Central American women understood the grief that accompanies motherhood and war. And the past evening, after they departed, they were determined to return and offer their support to Mrs. Hubbard on this important day. They thought of her as a lonely woman because those closest to her, her daughter and son-in-law, were selfish, incapable of empathizing with her loss. Juan's son, Eduardo, who on the previous day had prepared the fires, had volunteered to give up the afternoon and drive his grandmother and great grandmother to the farmhouse so they could attend to what they considered their duty, that is, supporting a grieving mother. Eduardo understood and also felt sympathy for Mrs. Hubbard. After all, he had lost both of his grandfathers to war. After their arrival, he occupied himself by tending to the fires in all the rooms.

"Yes, a good fire." Father Hilliard watched as the flames began to lick and crackle around the dry wedge of Oak. "I'll see to the other guests now and check back in on you in a bit," he told Mrs. Hubbard. "Can I get you anything before I disappear?"

He glanced toward the two stocky women sitting on the couch. Though many other mourners had come into the small reception room to pay their respects, they had all eventually left. Gabriela and Patella did not; they took up residency on the couch and did not move. Like the single candle flickering on the mantel, they shared a silent but intimate presence with Mrs. Hubbard.

"Just a tad more." Though she could already feel, just behind her eyes, the warm, intensifying tug of alcohol mixing with her medication, Mrs. Hubbard held the small plastic cup and indicated with a finger a ridge about three quarters of the way up. "Whiskey."

"Are you sure?"

"Please," she said, as Father Hilliard took the plastic cup out of her hand. She kept her hand raised, holding him in a position of servitude for a moment. She narrowed her eyes and looked closely into his face. He had aged a great deal since the last time he had forced himself upon her. They were in their later forties then. *Tom must have been in high school*, she thought. *How many other women of the parish had he had? Was it just the women or had he raped the boys as well, like the other priests in Boston? Is that why Tom had hated him so?*

She looked closely at his mouth and dull lips—she remembered them as brutal. He had forced them around hers and sucked while he jammed a tongue into her mouth like a frozen pop. The thought of it made her shoulders tense.

"Anything else?" he asked her before turning to the women on the couch. "And you two, are you all set?" He raised his gray eyebrows and cheeks in a friendly manner.

"Si, gracias," Gabriella and Patella waved and smiled. Although they did not know Father Hilliard, they suspected the worst. They had seen such men in their own culture, men of God who consider their actions upon woman, girls and even boys justified by their faith. And from the little they knew of Mrs. Hubbard, they also suspected that in her youth she had been an easy target.

A handsomely sized black man blocked Father Hilliard's exit from the living room.

"Hello, Father." Ezekiel looked down at the bald dome on Father Hilliard's head.

The shorter man lifted his head, bifocals balancing on the bridge of his nose, and peered over the top of the rims. "Hello," a thin voice barely scratched out of his throat.

"I'm happy to have bumped into you," Ezekiel said pleasantly.

"Oh?"

"I want to thank you for your kind words this morning at the burial, about Tom."

"Yes?" Father Hilliard tilted his head so that the ear with the hearing aid was closer to Ezekiel.

Ezekiel noticed the hearing aid and lowering his tone, spoke directly into the device, "This morning, at the service, thank you."

"Oh! You're welcome. Thank you. You are among friends."

Father Hilliard pulled back and cupped a palm around his deafened ear. Black men intimidated him. And over the years he had learned that he could hide almost anything, including fear, behind hearing loss. Besides, when exaggerating this disability he could usually shorten the length of any unwanted conversation.

Ezekiel spoke easily: "Thank you, Father." He had always been black, and Father Hilliard, he suspected, had always been frightened of blacks. This was not an unfamiliar situation. Ezekiel had met his share of scared, small town white men.

"I think you described Tom fabulously this morning during the ceremony. I also found it interesting when you said that in the course of human history, especially in war, it is tragic how stubborn men can be."

Pretending to have misheard, Father Hilliard squinted for effect, "Mrs. Hubbard? She's in here," he said loudly and then stepped aside to let Ezekiel enter the small room. "Mrs. Hubbard," he announced, "this man knew Tom from the war." Before Ezekiel could correct him, Father Hilliard slipped out of the room to refill Mrs. Hubbard's cup.

Ezekiel stood frozen in the doorway. Father Hilliard's trick had successfully confused him. He had had no intention of meeting Mrs. Hubbard yet. He wanted to slowly work up to an introduction. First, he had planned to meet Tom's sister, Elizabeth, and her husband Jon, and win them over, gaining their friendship and support. And then they could introduce him to Tom's mother.

Since arriving at the reception however, Elizabeth and Jon remained busy managing the unexpectedly large crowd. So he intended to wait until later in the day when the crowd thinned, wanting his time with the family to have significance to them and at the same time have significance to him. His greatest desire for the day was to leave with a feeling of closure. After all, over the last ten years he had vicariously watched and secretly participated in the growth and change of this small family. In the end, he was losing more than just Tom.

Ezekiel winced, unprepared to meet Tom's mother. Conversations with Tom's old friends had been difficult enough. Like the proud husband he felt he was, he found it painful to refrain from explaining the exact nature of his relationship with Tom and hard to keep from bragging about his spouse. In truth, he even found it hard to hear Tom's old friends simply talk about Tom.

For example, he was surprised when introducing himself to Ted and Shelly Dorsey, whom he had always assumed at least knew he existed. But they responded blankly: they had never heard his name before. Then, instead of explaining his partnership with Tom, he simply stated he had known Tom in Arlington. To which Shelly Dorsey took the opportunity to expound upon her own closeness to Tom, telling Ezekiel about Tom's "free spirited life," his "shoot from the hip honesty," and his "success and heroics in war." Until finally, hushing her voice, she recapped Tom's last phone call to her and Ted: He called them shortly before he went back over, she whispered.

Ezekiel knew that almost everything Shelly Dorsey told him was a fabrication. Still, he felt pangs of jealousy at the professed closeness they had. He tried to reassure himself that Tom's old friends merely needed to fill an empty shell of what they called "Tom Hubbard" with their own wishes. Without actually knowing Tom, they concocted a fantasy of him and their friendship, making him into what they wanted a friend of theirs to be. Ezekiel understood this. Still, each conversation had left him a little more disheartened and discouraged than the last. And he figured that if this is how he reacted to talking with Tom's old friends, then meeting Tom's family was going to be a heart wrenching challenge.

After Father Hilliard left, Mrs. Hubbard leaned her head back and looked over her shoulder. She only caught a hint of Ezekiel's presence in the doorway. "Come in, please. Come in," she waved toward a chair by the couch. "Sit." Her weak voice carried no strength; it seemed to drift meekly around the room and then fall apart.

Confronted with a decision that he had hoped to avoid until later in the day, Ezekiel hesitated: *Should I tell her who I am?* Again noticing the black shawl he had purchased, packaged and sent—it hung off of Mrs. Hubbard's arm and over the side of the chair—he wanted to touch it, to feel the familiar fine threads of the fabric.

"I hope I'm not disturbing you?"

His eyes lingered on the sheen of the shawl's shimmering gold fringe. It reminded him of Tom and how he had looked during their lovemaking the evening he mailed the shawl to Mrs. Hubbard. It was their last intimate time together before Tom returned to the war. As his face had twisted during the height of ecstasy, his tense white skin seemed to shimmer in their bedroom light.

No, he wouldn't tell her. His and Tom's love would remain hidden. Unlike Elizabeth and Jon, whose children served as a testimony of their fertile love, he had nothing, no proof of his and Tom's relationship and thus, he felt, he could never tell Mrs. Hubbard. *Why would she believe that Tom was as much my life partner as Elizabeth is Jon's?*

"Buenos dias." Ezekiel forced a half smile while trying his Spanish with Gabriella and Patella.

Should I?

Avoiding the subject of he and Tom would be equivalent to lying.

And why not lie?

After all, lying had formed Ezekiel's identity for half of his life. He had learned to talk around his sexual and romantic urges as a boy. As a teenager he simply dodged the subject. And as a young man, when he finally told his family the truth about his homosexuality, instead of acceptance they shut the door in his face. So to save his partner from suffering the same pain, he had agreed to go along with this charade, that is, he agreed to honor Tom's request to keep their relationship hidden from Tom's family.

Why should circumventing the truth now with Mrs. Hubbard be any different? He could always speak about Tom the way others at the reception had, superficially and in fabricated ideals.

But Ezekiel knew Tom through and through. He knew Tom ate a half a cup of oatmeal with a handful of walnuts each morning for breakfast. He knew it took Tom exactly four minutes to shave after his shower. And he knew how many boxes of Kleenex Tom bought every week when he did their food shopping on Friday's after work. Lying to Mrs. Hubbard about his partnership with Tom would belittle everything that their life as a couple had meant to him. Why should he continue to deny the truth of their love? Was it merely to preserve the lie that his partner had insisted upon? Yes.

But what good reasons remain now? After all, Tom Hubbard was dead.

"I hope I'm not intruding."

"Oh, don't be silly." Mrs. Hubbard's voice sounded far away, dreamy. "Please, take a seat. I want to meet all of Tom's friends."

Chapter Twenty

Melanie learned a long a time ago that drinking had an unfavorable effect on her. But she still flirted with the idea that when used as a social lubricant alcohol had its benefits, and that perhaps, at times, one drink wouldn't necessarily hurt.

Though in truth, many times her own life experiences had proven her wrong.

By her mid-twenties, she was already traveling down the path of a drunkard. In fact, before her mother died, one of their last conversations was about the drinking. Her mother insisted that Melanie had inherited her "love for the bottle" from her father. "That man drank with determination," she'd said. "Like you."

Now, at her cousin's memorial reception, Melanie decided to have only one beer, just to loosen the tongue, smooth out conversational nerves, and fit in.

She sipped the beer. Its bitterness expanded in her mouth. It tasted just like yesterday, even though it had been two years since her last drink.

Looking out the rain spotted window, she watched the mourners in the driveway as they huddled with jackets over their heads, smoking cigarettes. One couple waved good-bye and pulled up hoods before scurrying down to the street. Melanie's attention shifted back into the room when she saw in the window's reflection a short, bald man approach the bar where she was drinking. Recognizable from his dome, glasses and collar, Melanie had hoped to steer clear of him. Apparently that was impossible, so she simply hoped he would not notice her.

Father Hilliard spotted Melanie's boxy shoulders and hair and recalled her aunt's profile of years ago. That rectilinear look, like a figure drawing from the early twenties, had always attracted him. Before approaching, however, he pretended to busy himself looking for a bottle of whiskey to fill Mrs. Hubbard's cup. As he did, he brushed against Melanie's back several times. When she moved, he sniffed hard to catch the scent of her perfume. Then, letting the side of his arm rub against the bottom of her spine and the top of her behind, he enjoyed the sudden straightening of her posture.

"Excuse me, dear," Father Hilliard said and placed his hand in the middle of her back. Melanie pulled away and defensively turned toward him, ready to fend off advances. "Melanie!" Father Hilliard exclaimed. "I didn't recognize you. What a pleasant surprise."

"Father."

"Melanie," Father Hilliard folded his hands together in front of his chest. "I am so sorry. It has certainly been trying on the family. I must say though that your Aunt is holding up well under the circumstances."

He reached forward with both hands and wrapped them around Melanie's free hand. Rubbing it, he looked up and into her eyes. He relaxed his face into an expression of empathy and masterfully asked, "How are you doing?"

"Fine," Melanie said flatly and withdrew her hand. Averting her eyes, looking down at the beer, she wondered: *Did he know I stopped drinking? Who else might know? My brother, Tony; what would he say? Maybe Billy and Jeannine ... and Aunt Casey? But that's it, unless Aunt Casey told Elizabeth. Fuck, so what? And so what if Father Hilliard knows? Who gives a shit?*

"Tom will be greatly missed."

"Right." His touch lingered, almost a burning sensation . She ignored the temptation to wipe it off.

"I'm sure your aunt will be happy to see you. Have you spoken to her?"

"No, I just got here."

"She's asked for you."

Melanie shifted weight from one leg to the other as Father Hilliard leaned closer. The bar, window and wall behind trapped her. He tried to force her to look at him. She refused. Raising her head, she looked off to the left and focused on the caterer as he served her stocky cousin Billy Quinn and his wife, Jeannine.

Face reddening and jaw tightening, Father Hilliard examined her profile.

"If you want to talk about it, Melanie, my door is always open."

She wanted to scream, *"I'll bet it is!"* but she was unprepared for the amount of discomfort she still felt around him and she froze.

It happened one summer morning in the rectory after a church event, when she was eleven and her breasts, to her embarrassment, had begun to show. He had started by slowly massaging her neck and talking to her sweetly about how nice the day had been. Then he quickly slipped his hand down her shirt and cupped her chest. His deliberate hand was cold, wrong. She tried to scream, but her voice shrunk in fear as he enveloped her.

Later that night, ashamed of herself, Melanie went to her mother and told her about the Holy Father's behavior. To her shock, her mother said nothing and just looked at the floor.

"Times like these are trying for all of us, Melanie," Father Hilliard said softly, voice laced with concern. "Many of us find it helpful to share our feelings in order to come to terms with our loss. And, prayer ... prayer helps many of us, too."

He paused, hoping she would turn and face him. But Melanie continued to stare off to the left. He read her rigidness as an expression of anger at the situation—the war, Tom's death—anything but him. He had convinced himself over the years that she must have forgotten that time he'd had his way with her when she was a child.

Changing the subject, he asked in an upbeat tone, "Are you still living on Old Towne Road? I hear they've started building on those lots. I remember when your father wanted to sell that property off. It was a good thing your mother kept an eye on him. Your father, rest his soul, had many talents, I think. But money, or, well, holding onto money, wasn't one of them. You know, your mother, bless her soul, once told me that she thought you took after him in many ways."

"What about my father?" Finally, Melanie turned and looked directly at him. She had loved her father, and despite all his shortcomings as a man—a drunkard that couldn't keep a job, an unfaithful husband to her mother—still, Melanie played the dutiful daughter, willing to defend him to the end. More angry than intimidated now, she drank off her beer.

"I thought your father was a wonderful man," Father Hilliard said cheerfully. "At times you have his delightful temper. I remember that from when you were a girl."

"That's what you remember?" Melanie was flabbergasted. "You remember my temper from when I was a girl?"

"You and Tom, the two of you together, a couple of real fire crackers. You could really work all the children up into a tizzy."

"A tizzy?"

"I remember one Sunday morning, I believe Tom had served at communion, and, if I recall correctly, you and he had worked Billy Quinn into a froth. He was ready to—"

"You talking about me, Father?"

Billy Quinn appeared on cue holding a plate of rice and chicken. He offered Father Hilliard his free hand to shake. "Mel, you made it," he said. "Go see your aunt." Then, noticing the beer in Melanie's hand, he frowned.

"Hi, Father!" Jeannine said sprightly. She held a plate of chicken and salad off to one side and innocently allowed Father Hilliard to embrace her. "Melanie," she said, picking a fork off the corner of her plate and stabbing at a cherry tomato, "sorry I was so short earlier when Billy called you, but you wouldn't believe it, he drove through a humungous puddle and soaked some poor woman getting out of a car."

"No!" Melanie replied enthusiastically, relieved Jeannine and Billy had interrupted her conversation with Father Hilliard. *If there is a God,* she thought, *then someday the old creep will get what's coming to him.*

Chapter Twenty-One

Julian parked directly across from the Hubbard place in a spot that just opened up on the muddy shoulder of Quinns Way. Nestled between an SUV and a pickup truck, he peered through the streaks of heavy raindrops on the passenger side window. Moisture-laden white smoke rose from the farmhouse's chimney and then sunk and hung around the front yard like a light gray fog. To Julian, the old house looked haunted.

In high school Julian tried to stay away from the Hubbard's. Even though he had a car and lived closer to Tom than anyone else in their gang, he would usually talk his way out of picking up his friend. So when Tom needed a ride to school, to town or to parties on the weekend, Julian would instead convince Ted, the gullible one of their group, and the only other guy with a car, to retrieve Tom, even though Ted lived furthest away. And on the unavoidable occasions when he was incapable of finagling his way out of going to the Hubbard's, Julian would adopt a sour attitude and act as if he were performing one of the most difficult chores of friendship. This seemed strange, though, given the reception Julian got when he did show up to offer a ride. Mrs. Hubbard would hug and kiss him on the cheek and Tom's little sister, Elizabeth, would rush outside to flirt, encouraging him to show off his cocky, teenage posture. The problem was with Tom's father. Although, thankfully, Julian had never met the man, he was terrified of what he suspected.

Julian had a sixth sense for these things. When he was a child, before his mother remarried and they moved to Newbury, he, too, had been "pushed around." Same as a sharp cologne, he could smell it on Tom—the insecurity that came from regular beatings. He had detected the abuse almost from their first meeting in ninth grade English class. Though never spoken of, his intuition for Tom's hidden hurts helped to form a silent bond between them. Then, in junior year, shortly after Julian got his driver's license, before the willingness to drive to Tom's house had dissipated, he went to surprise his friend with a visit and his suspicions were finally confirmed.

That day, Julian remembered, had been an unseasonably warm Saturday in early May—shorts and tee shirt weather. Driving toward the farm, he found Tom wondering along Quinns Way with one shoulder hanging abnormally low, as if perhaps it were dislocated. Tom's head tilted to the side. He limped and looked lost, blue eyes swollen, cheeks burned red. His checkered, flannel, long sleeve shirt was torn from the shoulder. The tear allowed Julian a glimpse of the fresh bruises forming beneath. When he asked what had happened, Tom shrugged and said it was nothing.

Now, parked on Quinns Way, Julian peered up at the old weatherworn place. The rain continued and his nerves jumped around. He hadn't gone to the gravesite after all. Going alone just seemed too eerie. He reached to the floor of the back seat and lifted up a near-full, plastic half-gallon of vodka. Turning to face the tree line and stonewall that ran along the driver's side of his car, he said aloud, "Here's to you, my friend," and drank.

Cheap vodka gripped his gut and he held onto the steering wheel until the tightness passed. Climbing out of the car, he stepped into the thick mud on the road's shoulder. "Fucking farmland." Cinching his chin into his jacket's collar, he rushed up the driveway toward the house.

"Goddamn, the boy's decided to show!" Neil Bingham, smoking a cigarette, called out from under the portico.

"It's freakin' pouring out here. I'm gettin' fuckin' soaked," Julian shot back without looking up. He had recognized Neil Bingham's voice, and extended a hand as he slid under the cover of the portico. "Bing!"

They had barely talked or seen each other since high school, every five or six years at the most. But Neil grabbed Julian's hand and the two men folded into an effortless embrace, as if they had last seen one another just the day before.

"Can I get one of those?" Julian pointed to Neil's cigarette. "Left mine in the car."

Neil held the butt of a cigarette between his lips, closed one eye and, while the smoke curled up the side of his face, slapped a cigarette from the pack.

"Menthols?"

"Yeah, I switched a few years ago. I think they're healthier."

"You know, I quit for awhile."

"Oh, how's that working out for you?" Neil grinned, took the butt from between his lips and offered it to Julian as a light.

Julian, much thinner and shorter, appearing to be half the size of Neil, offered a narrow, sarcastic smile that reaffirmed their friendship. He placed the menthol between his lips and used Neil's to light it, inhaling deeply. A rush of nicotine flooded his brain, a white queasiness washed over his face and he coughed. It was his first cigarette of the day. He quickly composed himself.

"I tried to make the funeral and the burial but, you know, mid-week, man, and I work for myself. Sometimes it's just tough to get away. So, when'd you get here?"

"Ted picked me up at the airport this morning and then we did the church and the cemetery, now here. Can you believe it, man?"

"I know. Melanie called and told me."

"His cousin Melanie?"

"Yeah, you remember her? I already knew he'd been sent back over. She'd told me that earlier."

"She had?"

"She calls. We keep in touch. She here?" Julian looked to Neil, who just shrugged. "Anyway, she didn't tell me the details, but I guess it was a mess or something. One of those improvisational devices or something like that." Julian's thoughts started to drift, the nicotine from the cigarette making him suddenly sluggish. *It'll pass.*

"Yeah, I asked Ted and he didn't know either. You'd think he'd know, though. Christ, the guy still lives around here." Neil had lowered his voice, as if confiding in Julian, who stood silently beside him watching the rain.

Even though Julian was off kilter, he understood Neil's tone; Neil was inviting him to knock Ted. Ted was the easy target in their group. But Julian resisted the old temptation and let it drop, thinking instead of Melanie's call earlier in the week. Besides, the cigarette made his mouth dry, and his forehead began to feel as if something were tugging on it. He would need another drink soon.

Chapter Twenty-Two

From the portico, Julian caught a glimpse of Melanie through the dining room window. "You goin' in?" he asked Neil Bingham, tossing his cigarette into an overgrown yew.

"Right behind you," Neil said, tossing his butt into the sprawling shrub as well.

Julian pushed the heavy, black front door. As it opened, turned and looked at Neil for the first time since he'd hiked up the driveway. "You look good in a suit. Do you wear 'em every day?"

"It's the uniform."

Neil looked away. He knew Julian well enough to know that the underhanded compliment was really a slight about his weight. *So I'm not a high school athlete anymore. Big deal.*

Dizzy from drink, Julian spun around the edge of the door and made a grand entrance that appeared full of casual self-confidence.

"Julian!" Tony, standing in the entrance hallway, was genuinely surprised to see him. The two men embraced. "You look great, man! So, how you been? Glad you could make the long journey from—where are you now?" Tony had thought of Julian occasionally over the years, imagining him as one of those lucky people who had avoided adulthood.

"I've been in Lawrence for a while now and things are good. Hell, verging on great, I'd say." Then Julian paused for a moment for dramatic effect. Being a drunk, he was skilled at lying and manipulating, saying things in just the right way to get the effect he wanted. And although he was only partially-drunk, or half-drunk, or simply early-in-the-day-drunk, he figured he was not too drunk yet to pull this off. "Hey, man," he said, dropping his tone, "Listen, I just couldn't believe it when I heard. Such a shame, I'm so sorry—"

Tony unexpectedly choked up. "Yeah." His reaction was typically more staid when people offered their condolences about Tom's death.

"Mel said it happened in Tikrit?" Julian made sure his interest sounded genuine.

"Yeah, it ... um ..." Tony heard himself reply, but his own voice sounded hollow; it lacked its usual sugarcoated surety—"Tikrit, right ... that's what they told us."

Since the first newspaper article about his cousin appeared, Tony had had dozens of conversations about military strategies, military casualty counts, civilian causality counts and, of course, Tom's death. People approached him at the hardware store, supermarket, pharmacy and post office. He had received cards, emails and phone calls from old friends, local politicians, concerned clients and pesky anti-war types. Yet on all those occasions he treated the exchanges as if they were comments about the weather or a sports team. Even at the funeral and burial, and the day before when helping to clean out the house in preparation for the reception, he had brushed off Tom's death as if it were just another bad day. It was as if he expected to go to sleep at night and wake up the following morning to find all was right again—that Tom was alive.

Today, all day long, people had come up to him—*So sorry about Tom's death. So sorry about Tom. So sorry for your loss. You must be so proud.* Their sympathies left him unfazed. But for some reason Julian's comments caught him off guard and his knees buckled, his eyes closed.

Neil reached out an arm and touched Tony's shoulder. "Can I get you anything?"

Tony inhaled deeply, leaned his head back and murmured, "Get me anything?" Straightening, he forced a smile: "I'll be fine. Thanks."

"I understand, it must be hard ..." Neil said, as Julian grinned and slipped into the dining room, leaving him to deal with an emotional Tony.

Neil watched Julian slink from the buffet to the bar and then squat down behind Billy Quinn, who, with his wife Jeannine, was talking with the priest and Tony's sister, Melanie. In Neil's direction, Julian motioned *'Shhh'* with his finger to his lips. Neil rolled his eyes. *'No,'* he mouthed and shook his head, but Julian ignored him and sprung like a drunken jester, squeezing the Quinns together, pushing off the priest and reaching for Melanie.

"That guy's something," Tony said, lacking conviction. His momentary public display of emotion had left him wanting to hide. However, he fell into watching Julian and his sister Melanie horse around in the living room, until, "Shit—" he saw the bottle of beer in Melanie's hand and now he really wanted to cry.

There was nothing he could do about any of it, not Melanie, not Tom. Nothing, except stuff the pain into a place deep inside and forget about it for the time being. He turned to Neil and, in an oddly upbeat, carefree tone, changed the subject.

"Follow me, there's something I want to show you. The other day, under all the crap my aunt had in this place—You should have seen it, piles everywhere." Tony held his arms high as he entered the parlor to illustrate the extent of Mrs. Hubbard's collections. "I found a newspaper clipping of you, Tom and me. My aunt actually framed it. I must have been a freshman and you two seniors."

"Really?"

"Cross country, the division finals—remember? Tom won the 5k."

Tony stopped in the center of the room. Although he tried to forget the fact that his sister was drinking again, it was impossible. His thoughts drifted back to how sick she had been when he and Billy had found her hidden in her house at the end of the last binge. His heart broke that day.

"You look lost," Jon said as he spryly entered the room, placing a hand on Tony's back.

"Yeah, no, ummm—"Tony tried to compose himself for a second time.

Seeing Neil with Tony, Jon extended a hand: "Jon Goldberg, Elizabeth's husband."

"I saw you at the gravesite," Neil said, shaking Jon's hand. "Neil Bingham."

"Sorry. Neil here used to run track with us," Tony said to Jon. "Hey, remember the other day when we were cleaning and I showed you a newspaper clipping? Do you know where that is?"

"You'd have to ask Elizabeth. I don't know what happened to it," then to Neil, Jon added, "To look at this place now, you wouldn't believe it. I hope Elizabeth doesn't end up like her mother. She had a lifetime of stuff around here, a lifetime, I tell you."

"I'll check the other rooms. Neil, if I find it I'll show

it to you."

Tony left, but had no intention of looking for the photograph. After coming close to tears with Julian and Neil, and after seeing Melanie with a beer in her hand, it was time for a breather, time to get out of the house. He headed towards the kitchen's back door by way of Mrs. Hubbard's reception room.

"So, you went to high school together?" Jon asked, shifting all attention to Neil.

Throughout the day, Jon had slowly come to the realization that these people who professed to be Tom's friends knew very little about him. Jon and Elizabeth were no exception. They lived busy lives, and although Tom was family he had existed outside of their daily hustle and bustle. They regarded him more like an ornamental fixture that required only occasional dusting. Yes, Elizabeth's brother was duteous toward his family—he sent cards, mailed gifts and made the once-every-six-month phone call—but, as Elizabeth put it, "Tom preferred to live a quiet, private life." Well, Jon concluded after asking around all day, it seemed that nobody quite knew what this "quiet, private" life actually looked like. Maybe, finally, from an old high school friend, he would find out who Tom Hubbard really was.

"We ran track together, hung out, partied. High school stuff," Neil responded.

That answer was too vague for Jon. Maybe Neil didn't know Tom Hubbard either. "What was he like back then?"

"A quiet guy, you know, thoughtful ... a good athlete though."

"Did you keep in contact?"

"Yeah, sometimes. Not really ..."

Why aren't I getting any real answers? Jon wondered.

"Man, he could run though."

That did it. Right then and there, Jon decided that he would take it upon himself to piece together and discover just who *was* Tom Hubbard.

Chapter Twenty-Three

Mrs. Hubbard relaxed listening to the sound of Ezekiel's voice. His cool, low tone, his accent and the fluctuations of his syllables as they rolled from word to word soothed her. He sounded pleasant, like music. Her gaze drifted from the single dancing flame of the candle on the mantle to the pulsating purples, brilliant yellows and wondrous oranges of the fire in the fireplace. Induced by alcohol-mixed-with-medication, she had slipped into a near-hallucinatory world where shapes bulged and colors throbbed, amplified beyond their normal boundaries by a gold light.

Ezekiel studied her, searching the lines and wrinkles of her face for a clue that would inform him of her emotional condition or provide a hint that perhaps she did not believe what he told her. Her blank expression confused him—*Is she grief stricken? Drunk? Prejudiced?* At first, when he sat down in the easy chair opposite, he had referred to Tom as a roommate, then, as the conversation progressed, as a very close friend, and finally, his partner. But no matter how candid he was, she would only turn to him, smile, nod and say something useless, such as, "Thank you," or "You don't say?" or "God love you."

"Ten years." He took a risk, growing determined to explain the full extent of his and Tom's relationship. The more he pressed for her attention however, the more non-response responses she gave. He began to fill the vacuum with a fantasy that his relationship with Mrs. Hubbard could evolve into that of mother and close son-in-law. And that, in time, theirs could become as intimate a relationship as could be found in any ideal, loving family.

His fantasy placed him in the past, with he and Tom in Newbury for a visit. And this was his and Mrs. Hubbard's private time together when he could share with her his love for her son. In his mind, he envisioned them discussing future plans together—plans that even included adoption of a child. Yes, they had spoken of that, adoption, before Tom left for the war. *Next time*, he told her in his daydream, *when we visit, Tom and I will have a little one with us.* He visualized her looking at him as he spoke, her old eyes sparkling with excitement and joy. He would feel the warmth of her heart and love as she attentively listened to him by the fire.

His fantasy only went so far, however, as reality lingered in the form of Gabriella and Patella who sat silently smiling on the couch. Though their understanding of English was rudimentary, they recognized enough words in his one-sided conversation to get who Ezekiel was and what he was trying to tell Mrs. Hubbard.

As the fantasy ended, Ezekiel tried to control his mounting frustration. He longed for some form of substantive recognition from Mrs. Hubbard; if she would only look at him, acknowledge she had heard him. He pressed forward until he pointedly, almost angrily, told Mrs. Hubbard that he and Tom were homosexual. That they had lived as partners in love and life as much as any two married people would. Still, he received no response, save for a quiet, seemingly disinterested "Hmmm."

Ezekiel, lost in his determination, jumped as Father Hilliard unexpectedly appeared in the doorway. Looking confused at how closely the two had been seated, the aged priest stood holding Mrs. Hubbard's newly filled plastic cup of whiskey. Ezekiel pulled away from the old woman, unsure as to how long the Father had been there and what he had heard.

"How is everything going in here?" Father Hilliard asked as he handed Ezekiel Mrs. Hubbard's cup with a napkin on the bottom. "This is for Mrs. Hubbard, although I don't think she needs it. I'll be back to check-in in a bit."

As Father Hilliard left, Ezekiel's mind raced: *Did I just "out" Tom to the priest? What if he tells the others? I only wanted her to know the truth about her son: That he was loved, cared for. That I loved him.*

Standing there holding the dazed Mrs. Hubbard's plastic cup of whiskey, Ezekiel decided to try and speak with the woman again later, perhaps then she'd be more lucid.

"Hope I'm not disturbing you?" The muscular Tony smiled as he entered the small sitting room. "I'm just cutting through on my way to the kitchen. Excuse me."

"No trouble at all," Ezekiel said. "I noticed you around. I don't think we've met."

"I'm Tony Griffin, a cousin. It's good you could make it. I'm sure it would have made him happy."

"I'm not so sure," Ezekiel uttered, and extending a hand. "Sorry. My name is Ezekiel."

Shaking Ezekiel's hand, Tony picked up on his frustration and immediately felt uneasy. "Like I said, I'm just cutting through." Tony pointed to the opposite door.

"Did you say Tony? Tom's cousin? Tom thought so

highly of you." Ezekiel realized then that he had lost the relaxed, centered place from which he had hoped to approach family members. "Perhaps we can talk more later?" he asked, deciding it best to wait until after he'd calmed down. Though confused as to who this guy even was, Tony smiled and nodded. Ezekiel placed Mrs. Hubbard's drink on the small table next to the stuffed armchair in which he had sat and left for the living room.

"Tony," Mrs. Hubbard reached out and touched her nephew's arm, sounding as if she had just woken from sleep. "That black man was so nice. I believe he knew Tom in the army. He said they were partners ... that they served together ... that they were gay together and he loved Tom like family."

"He said they were *what*?" Tony asked.

"Has Melanie come yet? Would you ask her to come in and say hello?"

"Aunt Casey, what did that guy say about him and Tom?"

Mrs. Hubbard looked at her nephew blankly, her mind swimming in a fog.

But not missing a beat, Gabriella and Patella said in unison, "Novios."

Chapter Twenty-Four

The longer Carrie Phillips and her son Tommy stayed at the reception, the more guests she spoke with. And the more guests she spoke with the more she questioned her decision five years ago to let Tom slip away without taking any responsibility for their son. She began to think that perhaps she had unwittingly short-changed her child by letting Tom off the hook so easily.

The sad fact was, Tom died without his son ever meeting him. But, ironically, her decision to raise Tommy alone was the one thing in her life of which she was most proud. Single motherhood had changed her in profound ways. Almost overnight, when Tom abandoned her and Tommy was born, she changed from being a vulnerable young woman who gauged her self-worth by her ability to secure a man's approval, to being an empowered woman capable of making independent decisions.

Now, after talking with people at the reception, she began to re-assess her decision of raising the boy alone. It had been a selfish one. It was becoming evident that there existed a whole world in Newbury, that is, the Hubbard family, of which she and her son knew very little, if nothing at all. She started to think that her

Tommy should meet his father's family.

Not only that, but it appeared that at some earlier point in his life, Tom had inherited the open stretch of land near where she and Tommy had parked on Quinns Way.

That was Tom's land? she thought.

Carrie first heard about the possibility of Tom owning land during an argument. Actually, what she had witnessed was more of an ambush than an argument. Two older men, whom she gathered were Tom's uncles, practically assaulted a gentle, bookish-looking man in the dining room by the bar. They accused the man of land-grabbing, claiming that since Tom lacked a son to pass his land onto, the bookish man was swooping in from California with Tom's sister for the sole purpose of stealing the land out from under them. Unfortunately, that was all Carrie had heard because Tommy, tired from the long morning and frightened by the fracas, burst into tears. At the time, Carrie was more concerned for her son's immediate well-being than a couple of drunk old men ranting about stolen land. So she rushed Tommy into the kitchen.

The older men's words, however, had started her thinking.

Since that disruption by the bar, she had attempted, with little success, to lead all conversations in which she participated toward the topic of Tom's possible land ownership. But she was an outsider. And in a small town crowd such as this, the conversations kept returning to safe subjects, like her cute, attention-grabbing son.

"He is really something," Ted Dorsey commented as the boy walked around the living room engaging in what appeared to be a series of serious conversations with adults. "I try to encourage ours to be more sociable, but you know kids ... And, well ... I'm not the most out-going guy myself, so I guess, in a way, they take after me."

"Could very well be," Carrie replied, dismissively, eager to steer the conversation to her own interests. "This is really such a beautiful area. Your wife Shelly mentioned earlier, when we were talking in the kitchen, that you folks live in town?"

"Sure do."

"It's different than the city." Carrie, much shorter than him and unafraid of using her good looks, tilted her head to the side and, looking up, let a warm gaze settle directly on his eyes. She wanted him to feel comfortable enough to engage in the discussion of her choice. "Makes me think about how much I miss the country," she said. "Like just walking up to the house, by that stretch of open land back there. Was that a field, like for farming?"

"You mean down the street? It's a field alright, but I don't think it's farmed, maybe hayed. But it's the last open one around here. Over the other side, though, off Hay Street, there's the Trustees Land, Old Town Hill, the Parker River Preservation and there are still a few horse farms and haying fields and some corn. But the town is changing. Progress, progress."

"The Trustees?" Carrie suddenly envisioned the Hubbards as a wealthy hillbilly family, rich with trust funds and acres of property.

"The land conservation group? They're big— nationwide, I think."

"Oh," Carrie tried to hide her disappointment. "That field down the street, is that the Trustees' land, too?" She wanted him to answer, *"No, that's Tom's land, and now that he's gone who knows what will happen to it? If only he had a child to pass it on to."*

Instead, Ted lightly kicked the floor with the tip of his shoe. "No ..."

He had started to think about Carrie not as a mother

but as a single, attractive woman. This made him shy, and although he'd already spoken with her once before, slightly nervous. Nevertheless, he was curious enough to momentarily overcome jumpy nerves and ask her about herself. "It must be difficult to be a single parent in the city. Or, well, I guess there's probably lots of help—services?"

The question had come out all wrong. Wanting to simply ask what it was like raising a kid in the city, instead he ended up sounding like he assumed she had difficulties supporting herself.

"I'm sure there are plenty of services in Boston," Carrie answered, dismayed by Ted's turn of the conversation. "But Tommy and I, we get along just fine." She looked around for her son and lit up when Ezekiel gave her a small friendly wave from across the living room.

"Umm, Carrie," Ted said, nodding toward her son on the other side of the room.

Tommy had wandered over to the two old men, the same Hubbard brothers who had frightened him to tears only an hour earlier. The small blonde boy stood between the two curmudgeons with arms apart as if exaggerating the size of a fish he'd caught. The two men leaned forward enthralled by what the boy was telling them. Alley scratched his whiskers and Peter gnawed on an unlit pipe. The scene looked like an etched illustration or a Rockwell painting of a simpler time, an earlier era.

Carrie acted alarmed: "Oh no," she said to Ted. "Do you think I should get him?" In truth, she was pleased. First she'd let Tommy break the ice with them and then she'd introduce herself and finally, once and for all, find out about the land.

"They're really harmless," Ted said, taking a step

back to allow Ezekiel into the conversation. "He'll be fine."

"Well, okay," Carrie said, leaning toward Ezekiel, offering him a cheek to kiss. She was unsure as to why she did this; it just felt like the natural thing to do.

Without thinking, Ezekiel leaned forward to kiss her. The encounter felt easy and genuine, perhaps a result of their earlier walk to the house together. Whatever it was, they both noticed each felt a fondness for the other, the way old friends might.

Ted turned away, embarrassed by their kiss. He felt like a prude. Though he considered himself a liberal-minded Christian, tolerant of others—and open to public displays of affection when they were absolutely necessary, such as at weddings and funerals—a black man kissing a single white mother in a room full of strangers was beyond his liberal-mindedness, and so he excused himself, ducking out with, "I wonder what has become of my wife and children?"

"I haven't seen you since we walked in the door," Ezekiel said, straightening, towering over Carrie Phillips. "Did the little man find the toilet okay?"

"What a memory you have," Carrie replied, a charmed twist to her voice. "Yes he did, just in time, in fact. And ever since he's been the toast of the party."

"Good to hear he's spreading cheer. How are you holding up? How is mother?"

"She's good, tired but good." Carrie smoothed her skirt. Although the wet splotch had dried, she remained uncomfortable. The discomfort, however, was more psychological than physical. "I still haven't seen Tom's mother. I met her at the gravesite, but I was hoping to, well, say something more to her."

"I just came from talking with her," and, sheilding his mouth, Ezekiel whispered into Carrie's ear, "She seems out of it, like she's not even there. She's really quite bereaved. Yes, bereaved ... I think."

"That's sad."

Ezekiel's eyes widened and pulling back he mouthed the words, "... and stoned."

"Really?" Carrie replied with more breath than sound. As she did, Tommy's distinctive cry of distress rose again. Cringing at the sound, she turned to see the two old Hubbard men standing over her son. Concern for Tommy overrode a temptation to laugh at the old men's expressions. Their dumbfounded faces displayed how clearly shocked and disturbed they were by the boy's outcry. Carrie marched over and squatted in front of the boy, ignoring the Hubbard brothers. Ezekiel followed.

"What's wrong Tommy?" she asked in a motherly voice.

"Ma'am, we didn't mean nothing by it, seriously. The boy just started crying." Peter Hubbard shook his head and nervously twisted the bowl of his unlit pipe.

Frowning, Alley Hubbard repeatedly stroked his mustache. "Just started crying, just like that," he said, backing up his brother's story that the boy's crying had been totally unprovoked.

Carrie lightly wiped the tears from the boy's cheeks.

"You must have said something." Ezekiel felt real concern for the boy's well being.

"Nothin'! Nothin' that woulda made him cry, anyway," Peter Hubbard spoke slowly, deliberately. He tried to sound sober, even though he had been drinking all day.

"Nothin'!" his brother Alley agreed.

Carrie's silence held the brothers hostage. Although she winked to Ezekiel to let him know that Tommy was fine, she made the two old men wait through an entire uncomfortable minute while she coddled Tommy. Then, looking up at them, she sternly demanded, "What were you talking about?"

"It's just that Tom, our nephew ... " Peter Hubbard said, putting the pipe back in the corner of his mouth. "See, we were his uncles, and this little one reminded us of him. Could be like he was family or something."

"Well," Alley Hubbard added, talking to his brother, "then you told him Tom died in the war. That's when he started crying."

"You listening to their stories, Tommy?" Carrie asked the boy. "Did the stories frighten you? They weren't talking about you, you know. They were talking about another Tom."

Tommy frowned. His tears were already passing. Other people in the room were now catching his attention. Standing, Carrie stopped brushing Tommy's hair and he immediately wandered away.

"You were Tom's uncles? Hold on, don't tell me," Ezekiel said, putting up his hands like two stop signs. "You're Peter Hubbard, the older, and you're Alley Hubbard, two years younger? Pleased to meet you. My name is Ezekiel, and this is Carrie, the little one's mother."

"I'll be damned. How did you know all that?" Alley Hubbard exclaimed.

"Tom and I were close," Ezekiel proudly replied, and although he couldn't remember Tom ever uttering a kind word about them, he enthusiastically offered a hand.

"You must have been," said Peter reaching for Ezekiel's hand, "cause, we're kinda outside of the family."

"But Tommy always liked us," added Alley, still twisting the side of his mustache. He shook Ezekiel's hand and looked over at Carrie, surveying her up and down through the haze of eyes blurred with drink.

Suddenly self-conscious, Ezekiel realized he might have said too much, calling the brothers by their names and citing their ages the way he had. He excused himself.

"Right, which is why *that* should be ours," said Peter, ignoring Ezekiel's departure and nodding his head toward the window. Taking the pipe from his mouth, he returned to his chair. Alley watched his brother and then followed the old man's lead and sat down, too.

"What should be yours?" Carrie asked as she rubbed her hands together, warming them.

"That field down the end of the street," Peter Hubbard complained. "It was Tom's, and now if this damn family don't go and screw us out of another inheritance, it'll be ours. We ain't waitin' to die for nothin'—we're waitin' 'til things get set straight around here."

Chapter Twenty-Five

At the beginning of the reception, after the long black limousine slipped away and Elizabeth and Jon situated Mrs. Hubbard in her cushy armchair by the fire, Elizabeth tried her best to remain the central figure of the day. She moved from mourner to mourner, graciously accepting their condolences and compliments, and, when the situation called for it, showed the appropriate amount of grief and gratitude. Her personality seemed tailor-made for this type of event. She was even more alive and vibrant than when playing the role of Mother-in-Charge at her children's preschool events. However, when she bumped into her high school classmate and sometime-teenage best-friend, Shelly Harrison, now Shelly Dorsey by marriage, she found herself in a conversation that challenged this role as star hostess.

When Elizabeth and Shelly first saw each other in the entrance hallway, they shrieked in a girlish fashion that made the Dorsey children, Teddy and Tammy, gawk in awe at their mother and stick their fingers in their mouths for comfort. When Shelly introduced her "blessed little darlings" to Elizabeth and then explained to them that she'd known Elizabeth, "practically my whole life," the children's eyes grew even wider. Though the two women's relationship was incomprehensible to them, they knew that something important had just happened for their mom.

After the introductions, Elizabeth hugged Shelly, somewhat stiffly, and Shelly, somewhat reluctantly, allowed her to do so. They delayed a longer conversation until later, as Shelly thought it more appropriate for her family to speak with Mrs. Hubbard first. Elizabeth thought Shelly's idea "brilliant" and said they could catch up in a bit.

At least an hour and a half passed before they saw each other again. When Shelly finally sashayed up to Elizabeth in the dining room, Elizabeth was in the middle of telling the caterer, Arnaldo, that it was his responsibility to keep an eye both on the portions and on the number of guests lining up to eat, and that even though the turn-out was larger than had been anticipated, if he paid closer attention there would be enough, as she had certainly, most certainly, ordered ample food. Shelly, standing next to Elizabeth, emphatically agreed and then, with a flip of a wrist and cock of the hip, fell into a conversation with her old high school friend.

Elizabeth, who hardly drank, filled two real wine glasses with Chablis, one for each of them, and then she and Shelly leaned against the glass door cabinets in the access hallway between the kitchen and the dining room. They became tollbooths on a thoroughfare between the two rooms. The wine loosened their tongues, and as mourners passed back and forth, they celebrated their private conversation in a public arena. Like a high school clique of two, they shot intimidating glances at anyone who contemplated the rudeness of eavesdropping. And when they finished their first glasses of wine, it was Shelly who suggested they refill them.

Halfway through their second glass, however, the romantic memories that had so quickly rekindled an old friendship were swiftly swept away by the divisions that had kept each of them from contacting the other for wedding celebrations, children's births and parental deaths. The topic slid into dangerous waters—childrearing. Shelly, trying hard to sound intelligent, spoke about the important influence a safe community and a strong church membership had on her and Ted's decisions regarding raising their kids.

"When it comes down to it," Shelly said, lowering her voice for impact, "we want Teddy and Tammy to have the same opportunities that we had as kids. Newbury's a good town; the schools are good, our family's around. Over all, Elizabeth, I know you didn't go to church much when you were younger, but you have to admit, our church and Father Hilliard are a good influence on the children. Think of it, Liz, he and the church and the town all turned out today to support your family—and for Tom, of course."

"Give me a break." Elizabeth sipped her wine. "I'm sure. They came because they were curious and because we put out a great spread. And we're paying plenty for it." She tipped her wine glass to indicate their hospitality. "And *this town*—ha!" she said with breathy disgust.

"'This town'?" Shelly repeated, insulted by Elizabeth's tone. Then, composing herself, she tried to speak in a more dignified manner: "This town's grieving for the loss of your brother, our hero."

Elizabeth looked at Shelly, cock-eyed. "Pa-lease, Shelly, you don't really believe that, do you?"

"I do." Shelly stepped back and placed her glass of wine on a narrow wedge of shelf. She postured herself as if she were about to set Elizabeth straight. "When Father Hilliard got the word out, and the newspaper got the word out, we came together as a community to support you and your family. That's what I'm talking about."

Shelly tried to remain calm as she defended her hometown, yet old resentments were being dusted off in her mind and she couldn't help but think, *Those damn Hubbards, same as they've always been—ungrateful!* "No matter what you think, Elizabeth, people do care."

Elizabeth gasped before she spoke. "Father Hilliard?" she exclaimed. "The newspaper? Look—" she shoved a polished finger in the air in Shelly's direction, "when Tom left this town—after our father drove him away—nobody gave a shit then. Did Father Hilliard rush out to help Tom then? Did 'the community'? The only way he was coming back here to stay in this oh-so-supportive town was just how he did, in a fucking box. And," she added under her breath, "a box compliments of the U.S. military."

"I can't believe you just said that," Shelley replied, horrified. "Elizabeth, you are so jaded. What your brother did was heroic, and if you are too fancy and blind to see that, then too bad, but you shouldn't take it away from the rest of us. This town is proud of Tom Hubbard, our hero. And like your brother did, some of us believe in America and God."

"My brother! What do you know about my brother?" Elizabeth hissed. "My brother simply liked to play army—ever since he was a little boy."

Shelly backed down, growing frightened of Elizabeth's rage. Yet she was also satisfied; she had sufficiently offended her old friend. "I'm sorry, Elizabeth. I don't know, I don't know. This must hurt and I'm sorry." Shelly opened her arms and body to Elizabeth, readying herself for a show of affection, perhaps even a genuine hug this time. "This must be so hard on you."

Elizabeth's face turned to stone. Only her eye shadow and perfectly-lined red lips showed signs of color. *America and God,* she fumed to herself. *What God? Shelly's much adored priest? The asshole who touched me when no one was looking ... Who gave a shit then? Is that what God wanted? And my father, who regularly beat my brother— was that God's doing, too? Everyone knew what was happening in our house and no one did anything. Is that a caring, supportive community? As for America, America and its fucked up war killed my brother.* She held herself tight, but she wanted to scream, *How's that Shelly Dorsey? Good enough for you and your fucking "community"?*

"Elizabeth," Shelly said quietly, still waiting for a response to her open arms, "I'm so sorry if I offended you during this time of mourning. Can you find it in your heart to forgive ..."

Elizabeth looked past Shelly and stared at a stack of pasty old blue plates on a shelf in the cabinet in front of her. She studied the thick grime on the glass in the corners of the inside frame of the cabinet doors and wondered if it was new grime or if it was the exact same grime that, as a girl, she had focused on so deliberately when her mother pleaded with her drunken father not to beat her brother. She'd hide in this cut-through between the dining room and the kitchen, as it was rarely used, and wait for the inevitable—the distinctive snap of a belt or thump of a fist.

Elizabeth's eyelids fluttered. She moved her mouth, about to speak, but stopped, hesitated, then tried again. On her third attempt she spoke softly, "I think I'll check on my mother."

Chapter Twenty-Six

Julian wanted his old high school friend, Ted Dorsey, to accompany him and Melanie when they went in to pay their respects to Mrs. Hubbard. Although Julian was fond of Mrs. Hubbard, he feared that if he went in to see her alone she would smell the alcohol on his breath and confront him about his drinking. Out of all the people he knew at the reception, he figured she would be the one who would know he was half-drunk. She had called him on it once before, shortly after high school graduation, on one of his rare visits with Tom at the farmhouse. She asked him why he drank so much and then told him, "A drinking life leads to nowhere but misery."

Despite the overwhelming number of people who had given him similar warnings, his own mother included, it was Mrs. Hubbard's simple, direct words from over fifteen years ago that haunted him. So he needed Ted to join him and Melanie for additional reinforcement—two people to hide behind, confusing Mrs. Hubbard, throwing her off her game so she wouldn't confront him.

Julian and Melanie cornered Ted, his back against the buffet table. "You have to come in with us," Julian insisted. "It will be like old times, like we came to pick up

Tom or something. You know, like we used to."

Ted swallowed hard, Adam's apple bouncing as he spoke: "I don't think it's appropriate."

Melanie nudged Julian, signaling she wanted him to ask Ted again. She needed additional cover as well. *Julian alone wasn't enough*; worrying Aunt Casey would spot the insidious glow of alcohol on her in mere seconds. Moreover, Melanie suspected that because she had avoided Aunt Casey for weeks now—actively since the news of Tom's death—her aunt was likely already suspicious that the drinking had started again. Melanie did not want to disappoint Aunt Casey, especially given how proud Mrs. Hubbard had been about the two years of sobriety. *Best to hide it, best to prevent Auntie from suffering further troubles*.

Julian responded to Melanie's nudge and pushed Ted. "Sure it's appropriate; old friends going in to pay their respects together. Makes perfect sense."

"I've already visited her with my family."

"For old times," Melanie begged.

"No, you two should go in together without me." Ted sidestepped along the buffet table away from the pair, uncomfortable with their obvious reluctance to see Mrs. Hubbard on their own.

"Alright, then we'll just go in," Julian said definitively, shifting his weight from side to side.

Melanie swayed with him.

They shared a closeness that had just re-blossomed over drinks.

Arnaldo, the caterer, asked if they were in line.

Julian and Melanie smiled at one another and Julian answered "No" for them.

Ted, still nearby, looked down at the wide-board pine floor. He was sure Julian was buzzed, but he began to suspect that Melanie was, too. He had known her since she was a girl. She was one of those people whose personalities clicked on like a light switch and became extra alive when she put alcohol in her body. And now, with Julian on her arm, she was positively radiant. *Was it the alcohol or Julian or both?* Ted wondered.

Ted heard the town gossip from his wife. There had been a car accident, an arrest for drunk driving, and then lawyer fees and gambling debts that forced Melanie to sell the land across the street from her house. He heard all of that was in the past—he thought she was on the straight and narrow now. But maybe not.

The door swung open and Elizabeth marched through the dining room with her arms folded tightly across her chest. She disappeared into the entrance hallway.

"What's wrong with her?" Melanie asked.

"Right, let's talk to your cousin first—maybe she'll join us?" Julian said, speaking into Melanie's ear through her black hair. "You smell beautiful," he added with a husky whisper.

An exciting chill rushed up her spine. She leaned in and whispered back into his ear the only thing she could think of to say. "Did you see her? She's such a snit. Always has to be the center of everything. *Oh, look at me. I'm the most important person in the room.*"

Julian forced a laugh.

Ted, embarrassed by their exchange, moved further away from the lovebirds. At the makeshift bar he nodded "hello" to a casually-dressed middle-aged couple who were debating whether or not to have another drink or just leave. Much of the earlier crowd had already left. In fact, when the couple finally chose to depart, Ted noticed that the dining room was practically empty of mourners. Arnaldo gave his assistant a knowing look and without a word they began to cautiously remove the last of the steaming, silver food trays from the buffet.

Just then, Tony poked his head into the dining room from the kitchen access hallway and issued a directive before ducking back out again. "Mel," he said, "get your shit together and go see Aunt Casey already."

"Fuck him," Melanie whispered to Julian. As much as she hated being told what to do, she resisted the urge to respond loudly and defensively to her brother's order, even though he had embarrassed her in front of Julian, the one place she wanted to look cool. She guessed Tony knew she was drinking and wanted to avoid a family confrontation in front of Julian, who had no idea she had ever stopped. Melanie had neglected to mention it to him. In fact, during their series of late night phone calls over the past couple of years, she also neglected to mention any of the trouble that drinking had brought her.

"One more before we go?" Julian asked, guiding Melanie to the bar. He took two plastic cups and poured a couple of ounces of scotch whiskey into each. "That should do the trick." He handed one to her. "I'm a vodka man myself. But this is a formal event." Looking into each other's eyes they drank and gasped and choked together.

"Whew!" Melanie wheezed, setting the cup down.

She lightly gripped Julian's forearm as they navigated their way through the living room where Juan's son, Eduardo, who had brought Gabriella and his grandmother Patella to the reception to sit with Mrs. Hubbard, kept the flames alive in the large living room hearth. In the late afternoon light, some of the thinning crowd sat in little groups on the couches and chairs, chatting, while others simply milled about the long room. Melanie recognized most, but instead of saying *hello*, she tightly hung onto Julian's arm. She even ignored the two older Hubbard brothers who grimaced at her and Julian as they passed.

She enjoyed thinking that all these people—with their cozy little families and their sweet little children—could now see proof, in the form of a man at her side, that she had someone, too, just like they did. *You see,* she silently told the crowd, *I'm not alone either.*

Elizabeth stood in the doorway to the small reception room where Mrs. Hubbard sat, the back of her sleek black dress facing the living room.

"Hello there," Julian said meekly. He wanted to sound bold to impress Melanie. But Elizabeth's back, blocking the doorway, was daunting. Although they were close to the same height, heels made her taller and her overwhelming perfume and pure white skin intimidated him.

"Elizabeth," he said louder, summoning courage.

"Un momentito," she said without looking, turning only slightly and continuing to speak in broken gringo Spanish. She was busy negotiating, forcing, an hourly wage onto Gabriella and Patella. She wanted the older Latina women to clean the house instead of wasting their time sitting on the couch watching her mother for endless hours. The women were not interested.

"Just a sec," she repeated in English.

"Lizzy, let us in," Melanie demanded, to which Elizabeth finally turned around.

"Mel! And ... ?" Elizabeth had recognized Julian before when passing through the dining room, but now paused for added effect. "Julian?" she said with false surprise. "How are you?"

The thought of a friendly hug crossed both their minds, but neither leaned forward. Elizabeth could smell the cigarettes and booze on Julian, and Julian continued to shrink, frightened.

"I'm fine," he answered. "Under the circumstances, that is." He dropped his voice down: "I'm so sorry about Tom."

"She'll be happy to see you," Elizabeth said, ignoring the condolences. "She's always thought so highly of you. And Melanie," aggravation lined her voice. "Finally! I told her you were here, and of course she keeps asking, 'Where's Melanie? Where's Melanie?'" Elizabeth mimicked her mother as she waved her hands. "'Could you ask your cousin to come in?'" Elizabeth stopped and cupped one hand to the side of her mouth. "Anyway," she whispered, pointing to Gabriella and Patella with her thumb, "let me get these two out of here. I want to see if I can get this place cleaned up again before they go."

"Liz, you're such a brat."

Elizabeth shushed Melanie by raising a palm. Then, turning to face the small room and using both hands, she shooed the two older women off the couch and ushered them into the kitchen.

"What a trip she is," Julian said.

Melanie stepped into the reception room. Elizabeth's perfume hung in the air and mixed with the heat of the fire, making it difficult to breath.

"Auntie," she said, placing a hand on Mrs. Hubbard's shoulder. Julian silently slid into the room behind her and sat on the newly vacated couch.

Mrs. Hubbard's head fell forward, then suddenly snapped back as she caught herself drifting into a nap. She breathed deep and opened both eyes. The mixture of alcohol and medication was wearing off and things were becoming clearer. She could now hear the individual crackles of the fire as the sap sizzled in the logs.

"Auntie, are you alright?"

The old woman leaned back and looked over her shoulder. "Well, look who finally decided to come.

Melanie, dear, sit, talk to me. Where have you been? I called out the cavalry to find you."

"Auntie, look who I brought with me," Melanie said, stepping to the side to escape her aunt's attention.

"Julian, oh son, don't sit so far away. Please come here. Let me see you."

Julian remained on the couch. "I'm not feeling well and I'm afraid I'll pass it on to you."

"Oh, don't be silly," Mrs. Hubbard said, patting the arm of her chair and raising her voice. "How thoughtful of you to come. You would have made him so happy."

Her neck looked thin, old, and as she pushed her head forward to study him, her expression saddened. "Julian, it's been so long. I wish you weren't such a stranger."

"Unfortunately, it has been a while." Guilt grabbed his insides. Maybe he was just paranoid, but he was pretty sure she could tell he'd been drinking. Back in high school, when he did come over, he suspected that the hugs at the door were actually attempts to smell his breath. He knew that she knew all the signs—the droop in his shoulders, the cocky expression on his face and the overcompensation in his carefully articulated speech.

"It's really so nice to see you. There's a buffet in the dining room. Have you eaten?" she asked, eyes moving from Julian to Melanie and back. Neither of them would meet her gaze.

"Melanie, why haven't you called? Is everything all right, child?" Mrs. Hubbard tried not to sound upset but she was beginning to see that Melanie had been drinking. Her heart sank. "Are you alright?"

Melanie focused on the floor as she heard disappointment in the old woman's voice. Aware that her aunt saw past any attempt to use Julian as a distraction, Melanie suddenly felt naked, alone, and despite the heat in the room, almost cold. Her lips tightened and quivered and, covering her brow, attempted to hide the welling tears.

"Melanie," Mrs. Hubbard said softly, trying to see around her niece's hand.

She had suspected weeks ago, long before Tom died, when Melanie stopped the regular visits and calls, that her niece was soon ready for a fall—all she needed was an excuse. And if Melanie's father or her own husband were any example, Mrs. Hubbard knew that loneliness could be enough of an excuse.

She was at a loss as to how to help her niece. Experience had taught that once the drinking began anew she could only pray that God would intervene and relieve her niece from the madness.

Mrs. Hubbard looked again at Melanie and then Julian, allowed her head to sink into the cushion of the chair and, feeling defeated, closed her eyes.

Chapter Twenty-Seven

When Mrs. Hubbard opened her eyes she was surprised to find Father Hilliard standing over her like a concerned husband.

"Just resting my eyes," she said, using a phrase her grandfather had used when she caught him napping in the rocking chair in the afternoon sun. Now that she had finally reached her grandfather's age, it was her turn. "Sit for a moment, Jim," she offered, calling Father Hilliard by his first name. She motioned to the armchair closest to her. "Sounds like it's quieting down out there. You've been so helpful today, all of it—the funeral, the gravesite, the reception. Such a long day. I want to thank you."

Several strands of gray hair loosened from her bun and tickled the side of her face. Reaching back, she returned them to their proper place. "I was just thinking about how much this house has seen over the years. You know, my father was born upstairs in Tom's old room. And my grandfather, rest his soul—and don't ever tell Elizabeth this or she'd have a fit—but he died in her room."

"Your secret's safe with me," said Father Hilliard. Turning around, he lowered his old body into the chair.

"Oh, I know I can trust you to keep a secret." She

glanced up to the mantle at the single thick candle and the headshot of Tom in his dress uniform. "Both of us can, can't we? We've been doing it for years ... keeping secrets."

"Casey," the priest said, scrunching up his lips. An entire day of consoling people had worn the sage out. He was tired and wanted to let his and Mrs. Hubbard's past stay where it was, in the past. *What good could possibly come from revisiting our history?* His weary gaze rested on a bookshelf by the opposite wall. "You sound clearer now than you have in days."

"Strange, I've rested better here in this chair with everything going on around me than I have since the day he called to tell me he was going back over to the war." She tugged on the sides of the black shawl. "Well, it's over for him now, isn't it? Nothing left but us."

"God rest his soul."

"Yes, God rest his soul." Mrs. Hubbard softly rubbed both hands together and meditatively messaged each knuckle. She swallowed dryly; the medication and whiskey had left a soar paste in her mouth.

"Melanie stopped in," she said, looking directly at the fire, stretching her arms. "I'm afraid she's not doing so well. Do you know if she's still here?"

"I think I saw her go out the door with her boyfriend just as I came in to check on you." Father Hilliard removed his thick glasses and wiped his eyes. His age, the comfortable cushions of the stuffed chair and the heat in the room combined to make him drowsy and he yawned deeply. He could easily fall asleep.

"She was doing so well, too, before ... I was so proud when she stopped drinking. I was happy to see her feeling better about herself. But I could see it coming. Let's pray that this time it doesn't last long." She turned to Father Hilliard: "May God go with her, Father."

"God will," Father Hilliard confirmed. He yawned again and stretched. He was on the verge of drifting off to sleep.

"Jim, why don't you lay down upstairs and take a nap? The small room at the top of the stairs is open and I believe Elizabeth had the bed made. You can lie down for just a minute and rest your eyes."

"I should head back to the rectory."

"I'd feel much better." She reached across the space between their chairs and placed her hand on his arm. "You, out there, driving around at night in this weather ..." She let the words hang. "Is it still raining?"

Her arm, stretching toward Father Hilliard, blocked the path of a blonde, five-year-old boy who wandered in from the living room. The boy squished his face with disapproval just as Father Hilliard drifted off, head falling with a snort. Tommy dipped under Mrs. Hubbard's arm and presented himself before her like a gift.

"My, who do we have here?" Mrs. Hubbard recognized the child from the gravesite. He had been there with his mother.

"Tommy Phillips," the boy answered and stood politely in front of her, wondering what to do next. The boy's attention was immediately drawn, however, to Father Hilliard's bobbing head. The child studied the old man's nostrils as they heaved in and out, and he examined the Father's black and white tab collar as it disappeared and reappeared under his sunken chin. Mrs. Hubbard pushed at his arm to wake him up. Father Hilliard's chest jumped. His sleep-filled eyes opened wide.

The boy stepped back. "Are you the priest?"

Father Hilliard knew the boy had said something but even with a hearing aid children's high-pitched voices were difficult. And now, with his weary, sluggish head he had trouble focusing, too.

"Father, the child asked if you were a priest," Mrs. Hubbard said slowly and loudly. "Honestly," she added, playfully exasperated. She looked at the boy who appeared delighted that Father Hilliard was groggy and half asleep. "Upstairs with you, Father. Come on, I'll give you a hand." Mrs. Hubbard began to stand. The conscientious child positioned himself at her side, ready to assist.

"No, you stay, you stay," Father Hilliard scolded as he shakily stood. He breathed heavily and slumped at the shoulder. "Small room at the top of the stairs, you say?" He patted her shoulder as he passed on his way out of the room.

Without hesitating, the boy hopped into the empty chair as if he were settling in for a chat. "You have a nice house," he said. "Very big. Bigger than ours. Our building's bigger, but our house is smaller. It's an apartment."

"An apartment. How nice. Tommy, where do you live?"

"Boston."

"That's lovely. Do you remember we met earlier today?"

"Yes."

"Was that your mother you were with?"

"Yes, my mother. I think she's here somewhere."

He wriggled his small body all the way back into the chair and crossed his legs at the ankles. "You have a nice fire. I like fireplaces. We don't have one, but I like them, overall, that is." He ended the sentence as if he had just made an important point.

Tommy liked talking. He liked using words, big words, like adults used. From what he gathered by the expression on Mrs. Hubbard's face, she liked listening to him. As he talked, he covered all sorts of topics. For example, his best friend Arnie, "Sad to say, has an absolute addiction to thumb sucking. Overall a rather terrible set of circumstances."

He also talked about his daycare teacher, Ms. Jermyn, and how intelligent she was: "My mother is in agreement," he nodded. Then he mentioned that after daycare was when he was "most bothered" about not having a father, because that's when some fathers came, at the end of the day, to pick up his classmates. But his best friend Arnie, the thumb sucker, was without a father, too, and that's why they were best friends. But telling his mother about how not having a father sometimes bothered him would only make her sad, so he thought it best to keep that a secret.

Mrs. Hubbard hardly listened to a word the boy said. She caught only bits and pieces of things. Mostly she sat in awe, amazed at how much the boy looked like her own son, Tom, when he was a child. He constantly fidgeted and squirmed in his seat just like her son Tom had. The way he talked, completely unbridled, was the same way her Tom had talked. Along with her amazement, though, her heart ached as she listened. She wanted to hold the boy, to freeze him in time, to save him from growing any older. That way none of the things that had happened to her Tom could happen to him.

Perhaps he's better off without a father, she thought, blinking back tears. And in that instant she saw how their home had once been—the arguments, the fights, the hatred. She remembered her husband's hand hitting her Tom. He was a boy then, innocent, like this boy now. She saw her husband's open callused palm draw back and drop, slapping her little Tommy's tender skin until it burned red.

As she listened to the excitement bubbling up in the

boy across from her, she recalled how, in the end, when Tom finally fled their home, there was no joy left in his voice. But there had been once. He used to love crawling onto her lap and sitting there, snuggling, holding onto her neck and talking on and on about whatever came to his mind. She would wrap her arms around him and sway and kiss his blonde hair and listen. Tommy knew happiness and he could love—yes, he could love. He could love, that is, until the day the black and blue wounds hardened and he swore he would never feel anything ever again.

"Get away," he yelled at her one afternoon when returning from hunting in the woods with his father and uncles. She tried to comfort him, hug him, but he had been beaten, worse than usual. He was only ten. "I hate Daddy, and I hate you! Don't touch me! Ever!"

And he never let her hug him again.

I did my best, the best I could—she told herself.

The little boy, sitting in the armchair across from her, continued to ramble on from subject to subject. As he did, Mrs. Hubbard glanced at the photo of her Tom on the mantle—the resemblance was close—but not close enough. She wanted to rush upstairs to her bedroom, get a photograph of her boy and then hold it up next to this child's face and compare. Her memory may have failed in many ways, completely rewriting entire sections of her life, and on some days her illness controlled her so much that she slipped into delusions. But today, right now, she was crystal clear. There was no mistaking it; this was her son's son.

Mrs. Hubbard became agitated. *Where is that curly-headed woman I met at the grave? I want to talk to the boy's mother.* She tried to relax, knowing she should react differently, calmer. If she yelled out, caused a commotion, declaring this boy her kin, they would no doubt call her insane. But, in fact, she did feel like screaming, *I'm not crazy; this is my grandson!*

"Please," Mrs. Hubbard said to the boy as calmly as possible, "would you please find your mother and bring her to me. I'd like to talk with her."

Just as she spoke, she sensed a presence behind her.

"I'm here, Mrs. Hubbard." Carrie Phillips paused before stepping further into the room. She felt tension in the air and worried she had frightened the older woman. "Mrs. Hubbard," she said, "excuse me for eavesdropping, but I was looking for this little one and he seemed to be on such a talkative roll, I didn't want to disturb you two."

She offered the older woman a hand. "I am Carrie Phillips. I'm sure you don't remember, but we met at the cemetery."

"Of course I remember you. God love you, dear, of course I remember."

"Hi, Mommy," the boy said. "We were just having a nice conversation."

"Yes, how very adult of you." Carrie placed a hand on her son's head. To Mrs. Hubbard she added, "He's quite the conversationalist."

"God love him, he is." Mrs. Hubbard turned sideways in her chair to face the boy and mother. "I can't get over it. I can't believe it. God bless him." She ran her fingers over her own face as she looked from mother to son. Some of the boy's features were obviously from his mother, his mouth, maybe the tip of the nose and the ears. But the rest, the rest of his face was like her and her son Tom's.

Carrie began to wonder if she had made the right decision. She watched the wells of Mrs. Hubbard's eyes fill and guessed what the tears were about. Eerily, she recognized Tom's face in Mrs. Hubbard's. Not completely, there were some differences, but the elderly woman's skeletal features were the same as Tom's and even, Carrie now saw, the same as her grandson's. It was in the cut of their cheekbones and jaws, and the way those bones dictated the square shape of their chins.

She had never seen a picture of Tom as a boy, nor of Tom with his mother, or with any family member. She had missed the resemblance earlier, at the gravesite. But now, sitting near Mrs. Hubbard, it was unmistakable—these two were grandson and grandmother. Suddenly, she wished she had foregone the reception and returned to Boston after the burial ceremony.

Mrs. Hubbard instinctively reached out to touch Tommy. Trying to avoid the touch, the boy sank back in his chair, frightened of the strange look on the old woman's face.

"Yes, I'm very—" Carrie hesitated, unsure of the motivation behind Mrs. Hubbard's thin arms reaching for her son "—proud of him."

Mrs. Hubbard stopped reaching toward the boy and began to shake. "Stand, boy, let me take a look at you."

The boy's bottom lip quivered, yet without his mother instructing him to do otherwise, he obediently slid off the chair. Carrie thought then to remove the boy from the room, but she was too late. Before the boy's shoes could touch the floor Mrs. Hubbard smothered him, sobbing out loud, "Tommy, Tommy! Oh, God bless! God bless!"

Chapter Twenty-Eight

Since talking with Neil Bingham, Jon's curiosity about his brother-in-law's personal life only heightened with each subsequent conversation he held. It became increasingly apparent to Jon that although the guests were there to show their respect for Tom Hubbard, none really knew the man.

This was true even with those who claimed to keep in regular contact with Tom, like the Dorseys. They could offer Jon no more insight into Tom's life than what he already knew. Ted Dorsey first spoke to Jon about Tom's high school track achievements—apparently Tom won every race he ran his senior year.

Ted bragged, "Tom put our school on the map. A real track star."

Then there seemed to be a big gap in Ted's knowledge about Tom between high school and the present. But regarding the present, Ted knew for sure that Tom lived in Arlington, Virginia, and he was pretty sure, according to Shelly (she'd spoken with him more than he), that Tom had taken on a roommate to help pay the bills. But other than a roommate, Ted didn't know anything about Tom's friendships, outside of Newbury, or his serious relationships.

"He'd always been quiet about that sort of thing. You should ask Shelly, she'd be the one who'd know," Ted said.

But when Shelly joined their conversation her answers were just as brief, not to mention strangely curt and guarded. "Tom's a war hero and a very honest man. We are so proud to have known him," was about all she said.

Jon also talked to Billy and Jeannine Quinn, Tom's cousin and his wife, and much to his surprise, they knew less than anyone. There was the same basic information—high school track, the occasional family get-together, and then a confession of, "Really, come to think of it, we haven't seen him in years. But we tried to remember him during the holidays, sending cards and all that."

Eventually Jon came to the only conclusion he could deduce from the available information: Tom had deliberately kept them all on the fringes of his life, never saying very much about anything to anyone. Without more to go on, he started to think of Tom's life as cold and lonely. Perhaps Tom secretly suffered from depression or bipolar disorder, some chemical mishap in the brain, like his mother, and like Jon's own father.

Jon had just about given up trying to learn more about his brother-in-law's life when Ezekiel approached.

"Why so gloomy?" Ezekiel asked. "You look as though someone's just died."

The joke seemed terribly out of place, but there was warmth in Ezekiel's voice that made Jon smile. Still, not expecting to receive an informative response, he casually, almost absent-mindedly, asked Ezekiel how he knew Tom. And much to Jon's surprise Ezekiel responded, "I loved the man more than a brother. We were very, very close."

Jon was at a loss for words. He stepped back and gazed up at Ezekiel, who displyed admiration if not pure love for Tom—the man nobody else seemed to know. And with that, Jon understood that his brother-in-law had not only had companionship but possibly a deep and beautiful relationship.

"Tell me," Jon asked Ezekiel, "tell me about Tom," to which Ezekiel smiled a huge effusive smile and pointed to an open couch so they could both sit down.

Just then Mrs. Hubbard leapt out of her chair yelling, "God bless! God bless!" The little blonde boy she was making a grab for started howling, and the curly haired woman who Jon guessed was the child's mother, dove in to save her son. Thinking his mother-in-law had finally lost it, just like she had at their wedding, Jon ran for Elizabeth while Ezekiel grabbed the boy even before his mother could reach him.

Chapter Twenty-Nine

"**I** can't believe I'm telling you all this. When we left home this morning I told myself, 'Only the gravesite, Carrie, no further. I'll let him decide when he's older.'"

Carrie Phillips was perched on the arm of the stuffed chair closest to Mrs. Hubbard, who sat sideways in her own chair by the fire with an expression of bewilderment on her face. Elizabeth, who had entered the room not five minutes earlier, leaned forward on the couch, mouth hung open, listening with great skepticism to what Carrie Phillips had to tell them: The boy was Tom's.

Carrie angled her head toward Mrs. Hubbard as she spoke. "But somehow, meeting you there at Tom's grave wasn't enough. So when I heard the priest announce the memorial reception I decided we'd come, if only for a short time. That way, when he is older and wants to know more about his father, I can at least tell him— remind him—about all this, about all of you."

"I want to know everything about him, everything. He's beautiful. A beautiful little boy," Mrs. Hubbard said, glancing into the next room, where Ezekiel had taken the child. She was ready to be part of something bigger than herself. Bigger than the boxes of junk, the knickknacks and memorabilia, the piles of dishes and newspapers, the unused linens and silverware, all the things she had obsessively collected in the years after Elizabeth and her Tom had moved away. "I just can't believe it."

"So, why not before?" Elizabeth asked, more pragmatic than her mother. "I mean, why now? The boy's how old? Four and a half, five, you said? Why did you wait so long?" She pushed forward on her toes, slightly rising off the couch. "Besides, I can't believe my brother would abandon his child. Tom was even conscientious about our children; never forgot a single birthday, always thoughtful at Christmas and Hanukah. And even with you, Mother, that black shawl you're wearing, he sent that to you before he left. Correct? My brother wasn't someone who'd just abandon a child."

"Your brother wanted to abort this child," Carrie snapped at Elizabeth. Then, calming herself, she slowly exhaled. She knew better than to act on emotions and continued with a controlled voice: "I was afraid this conversation wouldn't be easy no matter when it took place. But Tom Hubbard, my son's father, didn't want this child, and I apologize but I thought I did what was right by staying away. Yes, now I wish I had done it differently. And I wish I had found a better way to tell you all about Tommy. But I didn't have time to prepare. I didn't expect we'd talk today. I had no idea how much my Tommy looked like his father when he was a boy until just now, this afternoon."

"That's it! That's all?! He looks like my brother?" Elizabeth yelled. "That's your only proof, his looks? And we're just supposed to accept that?"

"Hush yourself, Elizabeth," Mrs. Hubbard demanded without looking at her daughter.

Jon charged in from the kitchen and shouted, "You're here?"

"Yes, I am here," Elizabeth curtly replied. "Where

have *you* been?"

"Looking for you!" He sounded frazzled and out of sorts. The limits of his usually cool demeanor tested, Jon nervously sat on the couch next to his wife. "I've been running around the place like a chicken with my head cut off searching for you."

Jon was now completely confused because only moments before, when he was in the living room in the midst of the first enlightening conversation he'd had regarding Tom, he saw his mother-in-law leap off her chair and seize the little blonde boy. He was sure the old woman had finally lost her mind—a complete emotional break down.

"Wait a minute," Jon said.

"You've found me, so hush," Elizabeth said, attention fixed on Carrie.

"No, please, somebody fill me in. What's going on? Casey, are you okay?

"I'm happy, Jon. Happier than I have been in a long, long time," Mrs. Hubbard almost sang.

"Well, tell him," Elizabeth said to Carrie. But before Carrie could respond, Elizabeth, flabbergasted, turned to Jon and blurted out, "The boy is Tom's. Okay?"

"You're kidding," he said, and quietly added under his breath, "After taking to that black guy, I was sure he was gay."

Elizabeth glared at him as if he were crazy.

Jon swallowed hard, admitting, if only to himself, he was a little afraid of his wife's anger. Jon adjusted his posture to mimic that of his wife. But he stayed out of the conversation. His thoughts drifted as he looked over Carrie Phillips's shoulder and out into the living room. were the hefty Neil Bingham stood next to the even larger Ezekiel. The two men were looking down and laughing. *The boy must be entertaining them,* Jon thought and wondered if they knew they were playing with Tom Hubbard's son.

At length, Carrie Phillips, unable to suitably explain herself to Elizabeth, left the sitting room to check on her son. As soon as Carrie was out of earshot, Elizabeth tried to straighten out her mother and husband's thinking. In her mind, both of them were weaklings who had already unquestionably accepted a strange woman's claim and a child's facial features as proof in the matter.

"That's not enough, Mother. Just because you recognize Tom in that boy's face doesn't make him your grandson," Elizabeth growled.

"Elizabeth, stop it," Mrs. Hubbard replied. She turned to face the glowing embers in the fireplace. "I don't think your brother was as innocent as you make him out to be."

Jon sat silently on the couch next to Elizabeth. From his position he could see the top of Carrie Phillips's head as she stood next to Ezekiel. They appeared quite friendly. *Besides, hadn't he seen them arrive together? And wasn't it Ezekiel who had stepped in earlier and grabbed the boy from a crazed Mrs. Hubbard? And isn't Carrie out there talking with him now? Was this Tom's family—a little boy, a tall black man and a curly haired woman from Boston?*

"Please, Mother, Tom wouldn't abandon a child," Elizabeth defended her brother. "We need to see a birth certificate or make her get a blood test or something. Can't they check DNA? Something? Jon, you're a lawyer, tell her—we need her to produce physical proof."

"Hush, child," Mrs. Hubbard said. She was happy to suddenly have a new grandson and wanted to prevent Carrie and the boy from overhearing her angry daughter's skepticism.

"Mother," Elizabeth quipped, then lowered her voice to a snarl, "you know as well as I do that the tract of land sitting out there rotting away is in Tom's name and that it's worth well over a million dollars. If you think this pretty little gold digger is going to get it just because her son looks like my dead brother, then you're nuts."

"Elizabeth!"

"I'm not going to let it happen."

"Watch your mouth, Daughter."

"Jon, tell her!" Elizabeth demanded.

But Jon had other things on his mind. He was beginning to see that his brother-in-law had led a more interesting and full life than any of them could have imagined.

Chapter Thirty

A heavy mist and a light drizzle burdened the already dark November evening. "Was his father buried here, too?" Julian loudly called back to Melanie anxiously pushed fingers through his damp hair.

An ancient White Oak stood out against the colorless cemetery landscape. Julian, drunker and less stable than earlier, teetered cautiously over the slippery leaves that had collected on the grass. He thought of stopping to let her catch up. And if she did, he plotted to slip his arm around her waist and pull her close. Even bolstered by alcohol's courage, however, he worried she might reject him, so he continued moving forward instead.

"Everybody's buried here," she shouted ahead, trying to keep up. The drinks she had had back at the reception and in Julian's car on the ride over to the cemetery challenged her equilibrium and made walking difficult. She had already fallen twice, so not only was her hair wet but her clothes were as well.

"Whereabouts?" Julian yelled, now frustrated with her slowness. He stopped, lit a cigarette and surveyed the hillside, dotted with hazy gray marble gravestones. Then, just off to his left, on the top of a rise, he noticed a blue tarp over a rounded lump. He let her catch up.

Melanie had heard the frustration in his voice and felt the need to apologize. "I'm sorry," she said making her way to him. "I thought it was just here, not too far from the tree." She had recognized the big Oak; it marked their family plot. Upon seeing the tree from the cemetery road, she had suggested they walk.

"It's so dark, and the rain ... I'm sorry, should we turn back?" Her voice trailed off, hoping for his approval.

Julian inhaled several times off a cigarette and resisted the urge to slip an arm around her, still nervous about her reaction. But after seeing that his frustration held her in a different way, suddenly the fear of rejection disappeared. "Turn back?" he said, almost angrily, as if the suggestion was an insult. He remained silent, deliberately making her feel guilty with his obvious dissatisfaction, forcing her to keep all attention on him. After a moment, afraid she might notice Tom's gravesite before he could point it out, he announced, "There, over there, under the tarp; is that a pile of dirt?"

"That must be it," Melanie agreed, relieved.

Julian grabbed Melanie's hand and together they headed toward the mound.

Yards away, a sheet of plywood lay under another tarp that had been placed over a rectangular hole in the ground. "Holy shit," Melanie gasped, grabbing Julian's arm.

They walked around the perimeter of the covered hole. Although the plywood hid what lie underneath, they each felt certain that Tom's coffin and body lay at the bottom of the pit. Julian stopped at what he figured was the head of the grave. He stood in the spot where he assumed the priest had stood and delivered the final prayers. Melanie stood next to him, hands now deep in her pockets. The drizzle had stopped but the mist hung thickly over the site. Neither spoke.

Julian kicked at the edge of the sheet of plywood. Rainwater dripped from the tarp onto the ground. Melanie returned her hand to his arm to still him.

What am I doing here? he asked himself as he slid an arm around Melanie's waist. She allowed her body to fold into his and he felt the head of his penis twitch with anticipation. But he overlooked this sexual urge and tried to concentrate instead on how he thought he was supposed to feel at the gravesite of a dead friend. Something attuned to loss, is what he determined. But his body and emotions, reeling from years of drinking, had forgotten how to feel anything. Mostly, he needed a drink. He would cry later, he told himself, if he could, in private. He kicked at the plywood again.

"Stop kicking," she whispered, rubbing his arm lightly, almost flirting.

She wanted to be with him, like a wife, joined at the hip, sharing this dark moment together.

Gazing into the misty evening, she let her mind take her away from where they were and began to fantasize that this had nothing to do with death and dying—this was her and Julian's wedding. Her cousin Tom would be there, too, as Julian's best man. She could almost see a shadow of the shape of Tom's body positioned next to Julian. She fancied the rectangular grave a runway and the foot of it an altar. And the family headstones scattered about the hillside plot became the folding chairs at an outside nuptial ceremony. The mist and the reaching limbs of the Oak tree formed a canopy, an arbor and a tent. And there, smiling like the sun, sitting in the chairs, were her mother and father, her grandparents and relatives, relations she hardly knew and others she had never met. In a white gown with a silk veil, she eagerly awaited Julian's confirmation kiss. And Julian, in a black tuxedo with a light blue cummerbund, opened his palm for Tom, who, ring in hand, stood impressively in his military dress uniform, a shiny sword dangling at his side.

"Wow," Julian said, feeling an uncomfortable pressure created by their silence.

"Yes," Melanie responded, still dreaming. She turned toward him, her lips wet and parted.

Hoping he could manage to conceal his usual clumsiness with women, Julian opened his mouth and leaned forward, accepting her.

Chapter Thirty-One

Other than to refill their plastic cups with whiskey at the bar, the elderly Hubbard brothers, Peter and Alley, had remained in the same spot, under the large window in the living room, throughout the entire memorial reception.

"Tony!" Peter Hubbard called out to his nephew from his chair. "Tooooony!"

Busy acting interested in a conversation with Ted Dorsey, Tony ignored his annoying uncle. His attention, however, remained fixed on the sudden lack of activity in the reception room. He had heard from Jeannine Quinn about the commotion his aunt caused over a little boy. Now he was positive that his cousin Elizabeth and her husband Jon were in there, too, with his aunt, discussing what had happened—and they were doing so without him. He was being kept out of the family loop. On top of that, since he had started talking with Ted Dorsey, the blonde boy's mother had come out, retrieved her son from the black man he'd just met, Ezekiel, and Neil Bingham and then returned to the small room. His curiosity piqued, yet he would have to wait to find out more details.

"Tony," Peter Hubbard repeated. "Goddamnit, boy, I

know you can hear me!"

"Those highfalutin' Griffins," Ally Hubbard grumbled, calling Tony by his last name. "Never see our part of the family go around ignoring one another."

"Hey, Tony, you remember your Uncle Edward, our brother?" Peter Hubbard asked, words stumbling over the whiskey he'd been drinking all afternoon and the pipe that hung from the corner of his mouth.

"What?" Tony finally barked over his shoulder, fed up. "What the hell do you two want?"

"We was just talking ... me and Peter here," Alley Hubbard said, rolling the ends of his mustache. "Well, we wanted to know if you remember when us and your dad and our brother Edward and you and Tom used to take the guns and go out looking for deer, just out back here." Alley pointed in the direction of the new neighborhood that had been built on the Hubbard's old acreage.

"Jesus," Tony muttered and then tempered himself enough to civilly turn sideways to face them. This position provided a better angle to both observe the goings-on in the reception room as well as include Ted Dorsey in the reluctant conversation now beginning with his uncles. "Actually, you know, I had completely forgotten about those hunting expeditions. I must have been only six or seven."

"No older than that boy over there," Peter Hubbard pointed to little Teddy Dorsey who stood by the parlor doorway watching his mother struggle with the zipper on his sister's coat. Ted Dorsey shrugged his shoulders, excused himself from the conversation and went to assist his wife.

"That's right," Peter Hubbard continued. "We'd let you and Tom carry the shotgun shells, and you'd drop them as we went, leaving a trail."

"That's right, so if we ever got lost, we'd just follow the trail of buckshot," Alley Hubbard laughed and coughed and crossed his legs at the knee.

"Sure, I remember Uncle Edward," Tony said, referring to Tom's father. "God, he was easily ticked off; he could get mad at nothing at all. One time—I haven't thought of this in years—one time it was real cold out, in the teens—freezing, but Tom still took his jacket off and made it into a sack to carry all the shells."

Tony cradled his arms as if carrying the sack of shotgun shells.

"Tom couldn't have been more than nine or ten. And he had to, well, he had to 'go' bad—I mean real bad ..." Tony changed his tone, as if setting up a familiar joke.

The Hubbard brothers smiled and settled in to hear the rest of the story.

"And afraid his father would get mad, he wouldn't trust me to hold the shells—I was too small. He said I'd drop them. So he held onto them, in his jacket, with both hands, as he squatted there in the icy woods." Tony forced a laugh. "But then he slipped and fell on this briar patch and scratched up and bruised up his ass—" Tony stopped.

Disgust washed over him.

"Wait a minute," he thought out loud. "That's not what happened."

"Tell it, Tony. Finish it up. It's a real funny story," Peter blurted out, laughing just thinking about it.

"Wait a minute. No," Tony said quietly. "That's not how it happened, Uncle Peter." Tony stepped back from the brothers remembering for the first time since he was a kid what had really happened in the woods beyond the haying fields that winter's day. There had been no need to "go," no slip on the ice and no fall in the briar patch.

He and Tom had been walking along the path,

picking up the empty shotgun shells that the men had discharged from their guns. And, as usual, Tom was frightened of his father's wrath, which could bubble-up at anytime for no apparent reason. So Tom, overly cautious, had wrapped the empty shells in his jacket so as not to drop any. Shivering in just his shirtsleeves, carrying the shotgun shells, Tom ran down the path to catch up with the men. Tony, so much younger, smaller, followed as best he could, but stopped a few yards away when Tom reached the older men. Tony remembered the furious expression on Uncle Edward's face when he turned from the other men and looked at his son.

"He's dumber than the whore he's come from," Tom's father had snapped. And then, as punishment for the mishandling of the empty shotgun shells, he demanded Tom undo his pants and drop to his hands and knees. Tony remembered climbing behind a stonewall for protection, while Tom, barebacked, was whipped by his father with a switch from a nearby Aspen tree. The other men, including Tony's own father, did nothing to stop Uncle Edward.

Whipped until his bottom was bloody and crisscrossed with red stripes, Tom was frozen, feverish and practically delirious by the time they returned to the Hubbard farmhouse.

On the walk back across the haying fields, Tony's father and the Hubbard brothers bore down on little Tony. They threatened him with a similar punishment unless he adopted a more humorous tale about his cousin's mishap while hunting with his father and uncles. And later that day, when his mother and aunt questioned Tony about the incident, he began to craft the story that he would faithfully repeat again and again, when asked about what had happened to Tom that day.

And that evening, when things had quieted down,

when he was still trying to make sense of the day, he asked his older sister, Melanie, what a whore was. She slapped him, and from then on he knew for sure—the new story was the only story of what had happened that day.

Now, thirty years later, Tony could clearly see that afternoon in his mind. He saw a frail, naked ten-year-old boy, his skin turning a pale blue as he knelt, crying and bleeding, humiliated in the center of a circle of men.

Tony looked at the old Hubbard brothers and felt ashamed. They, along with his own father, had scared him into keeping the actual events of that day so perfectly hidden in his memory that even today, decades later, he was ready to lie on cue as they reminisced about their hunting expeditions.

The Hubbard brothers watched Tony's facial expressions dance with changing emotions as they waited for the humorous conclusion of the story, the one that featured Tom slipping into the thorny winter bramble as he tried to hold the shotgun shells in a jacket while he squatting to defecate at the edge of the haying fields.

"Come on, get on with it," Peter Hubbard demanded. "Finish the damn story. It's funny!"

Tony remained silent. The thought of that day now sickened him.

"Told-ya he wouldn't remember the story," Alley Hubbard chided.

"What? You set me up, you bastards!" Tony said, furious with them and with his own actions; lying to cover for their weaknesses—*I'm no better than them.*

"What you talking about, boy?" Alley Hubbard spit out his words.

"You wanted me to repeat that bullshit lie about the day that Tom's father whipped the shit out of him in the woods while you piss-heads stood around, watching, practically cheering Uncle Edward on. I can't fucking believe it. I bought your shit. Christ! And even when Tom told our mothers what really happened—as if I hadn't seen it with my own eyes—I lied for you assholes. You stood there watching it all. That's what I remember. He was just a kid and you did nothing, nothing!"

"You don't know what you're talking about," Peter Hubbard said coolly.

"I know exactly what I'm talking about," Tony's anger had peaked and now he felt weak.

"You think you're such a goddamn hot shot, Mr. Know-It-All-Griffin. Well, maybe you're right. Maybe our brother had his suspicions about that boy's mother—about her actions. The point needed to be made and he made it—properly and with witnesses."

Peter Hubbard slid back in the chair and returned the pipe to the corner of his mouth, satisfied he had set Tony straight.

Alley Hubbard folded his hands over his belt buckle. "You see, boy, not everything's the way it seems." Then he pushed back and nodded to his brother with approval.

Resigned, Tony looked at the floor. "You're fucking sick. You're both fucking sick, you know that?" But his insides ached because he knew what they were referring to. When little, he had heard his parents argue about the same thing. And when he asked his mother about it, she hit him saying it was a lie: "That silly talk ends here. Tom's father is Tom's father, no matter what your daddy says."

Angry with himself, Tony moved away from the Hubbard brothers. *I was just a frightened boy,* he silently told himself. Through the doorway of the reception room he could see Aunt Casey's silhouette move about. He hadn't thought of any of this in years, not the abuse and not the doubts about who really was Tom's father. It had all seemed like a terribly foggy dream left over from boyhood, a nightmare from the past that had been forcibly rewritten as a comedy soon after it happened.

Chapter Thirty-Two

Jon trusted that his wife would at least try to act civil and watch her words while he went to talk with Ezekiel. In short, he hoped she wouldn't offend Carrie Phillips too much. He understood Elizabeth's concerns about a woman just showing up with a boy and claiming Tom was the father. And she was right to question Carrie Phillips's motivation—there was, after all, the land to consider. But when Jon saw the boy next to his mother-in-law and compared the two of them to the picture of Tom in his dress uniform on the mantle, the resemblance, although not exact, was uncanny. The boy's chin and cheekbones, the square jaw and even the corners of his eyes were a softer, youthful version of the man in the photo.

But if Tom was the boy's father, then who was this man Ezekiel? Jon wanted to learn more about Ezekiel's relationship with Tom. He also wanted to know more about Ezekiel's relationship with the boy and the boy's mother. So he excused himself from Elizabeth, his mother-in-law, Carrie Phillips and the boy, and slipped out of the sitting room and into the kitchen to find Ezekiel.

Although the reception had wound down to just

family and close friends, Jon decided he would still try to avoid any unnecessary attention. He hoped to keep this new family secret about Tom possibly having fathered a son quiet for just a little longer.

Jon walked through the kitchen and into the access hallway, pausing in the back of the empty dining room; the Dorseys were in the entrance hallway. He watched and waited as Ted Dorsey pointed to the living room as if trying to figure out if he'd forgotten something. His wife Shelly threw up both hands in frustration before pushing their two children out the door. Ted shrugged and followed after her. With the coast now clear, Jon crept forward into the dining room, satisfied he could avoid any awkward, probing conversations about the events in the reception room.

In the entrance hall by the front parlor doorway, Jon stood on tiptoes and stretched his neck to see over a couple who were pulling on rain coats and blocking his view into the living room. Unfortunately, this move attracted more attention than anticipated. Glancing down, he saw Billy and Jeannine Quinn looking directly up at him from the couch in the parlor.

"Looking for someone?" Billy Quinn asked.

"Well," Jon hesitated, "that big guy, Ezekiel. Have you seen him?"

"I did," Jeannine perked up. "He went out a little while ago. I said goodbye, but he said he'd be right back, just running out to the car to grab something. He's a nice man, isn't he, honey?" she chided Billy, who still felt rather silly regarding his earlier run in with Ezekiel. "Want me to tell him something when he comes back?" Jeanine offered.

"No, but thank you." Then, just as Jon returned to the dining room, the front door opened and in walked Ezekiel carrying a small knapsack.

"Just the man I'm looking for," Ezekiel said, placing a hand on Jon's shoulder. "I was hoping we would have a chance to talk more."

"Me, too," Jon replied. "How about the kitchen?" He wanted to keep their conversation as private as possible, and the only activity in the kitchen was Gabriella and Patella cleaning up, as per Elizabeth's earlier insistence.

Ezekiel placed the small knapsack on the cluttered kitchen table. "I brought some things to share with the family." As he spoke, Patella hurriedly cleared off the table, stacking plates by the sink and moving several containers with leftovers to a counter. Then, without a word, but flashing a knowing smile at Ezekiel, she returned to washing dishes.

"Thank you," Jon said to Patella, appreciative of her efforts, and then to Ezekiel, "I'd love to see them." Jon sat kitty-corner to where Ezekiel stood and with a determinant wave, as if with a client at the law office, invited Ezekiel to join him.

Ezekiel's size dwarfed the table and chair as he sat. "First, I really need to be out in the open. I loved Tom very much; we were partners, as much as any two people can be."

"I suspected something, but I wasn't positive that Tom was ..."

"Please, Jon, just let me talk," Ezekiel softly placed a hand on Jon's forearm, quieting him. "Where do I begin? Tom was a happy man, but a confused man as well."

Ezekiel stopped, held his breath, folded his hands on the table and began again. "Why am I telling you all this? Well, because I want an ally. You see, strange as it may seem, although you don't know anything about me, or that I even existed until a little while ago, I knew about you, all of you—Mrs. Hubbard, Elizabeth and your children. Each year I updated your Christmas-Chanukah photos on our refrigerator. I've watched you all grow and change. But it was more than that, really, I followed you for Tom, because Tom, in many ways, lost sight of things, like his family. Well, it was more than that, you know ... well, how could you know?'

Jon looked quizzically at Ezekiel.

"What I mean is, well, you see—Tom and I celebrated our tenth anniversary together just before he went back over. That's three years longer than you and Elizabeth."

Ezekiel let the words hang in the air, watching for any signs that Jon understood the point he was trying to make—that his loss of Tom would be the equivalent of Jon losing Elizabeth.

"Uh-huh," Jon said, missing Ezekiel's point.

"How should I put this?" Ezekiel continued. "Do I say that seeing you all today at the funeral and gravesite broke my heart? Yes, it broke my heart. But I respected my partner's wishes. Do you understand? You didn't even know I was there and yet Tom was the center of my life for the last ten years. Did you know we owned our house together in Arlington?"

Jon nodded slowly, it was a lot to swallow: Tom had had a life that the family had known nothing about.

"After the burial service, I watched you and Mrs. Hubbard and Elizabeth get out of the limousine. I was angry. I felt robbed of my rightful place. Tom was my life partner, my everything, and you people, whom I kept in contact with *for him*, got to be the public face of his family. It seemed so unfair.

"Did you even know who Tom was? Did you know that Tom was active in our community? Yes, he was a volunteer at a homeless shelter. And do you even know what he did for work?"

Jon hesitated. "He was in the Army?"

"He was a track coach, Jon, and a high school Phys Ed teacher. Did you know his rank before he died? He was a First Lieutenant in the Army Reserves. Or did you know that when he signed up he never dreamed he'd end up in an actual war? But he loved the army; loved being part of it. He loved the whole thing, loved being a soldier."

Ezekiel sighed. "But I realized something watching you all this morning. I realized that as much as I resented you for getting to represent him instead of me, as much as I hated it, I couldn't be angry with you, because over the years I have fallen in love with you, with this whole family. Tom's family became my family, from afar—do you understand? I'm the one who sent you cards and gifts. I'm the one who made him call a few times a year. Me. I know you don't know this, but I'm the one who picked out the knives for your wedding gift and had them engraved seven years ago. He refused to let me join him at your wedding. And, as you didn't know I existed, you couldn't invite me."

Ezekiel shook his head at the absurdity of it all, then paused for a moment before starting again.

"I am sorry to tell you this, but he wanted nothing to do with you people. He told me how much of an asshole his father had been. How he'd get drunk and beat him. But at times he spoke so fondly of his mother and Elizabeth—about growing up around here, on the farm." Ezekiel reached for the knapsack. "I have a black and white that he loved. It shows the empty fields in front and this house behind him. This area, the house, the farm, it was all there, present in the man I loved." Ezekiel took his hand off the knapsack and placed it over his heart.

The two men sat in silence until Eduardo, Juan's son, crashed through the back entryway of the kitchen with a load of firewood cradled in his arms and headed for the dining room.

"Cuidado! Cuidado! Careful," Gabriella called after him.

"My Tom carried some serious wounds. I often got the feeling that he was always fighting inside. But Tom was also a loving man. And I thought it was important that he didn't lose contact with his family. I had faith that he could heal. I wanted him to at least try. I knew he'd been deeply hurt. I also knew how much he could love and wanted to be loved."

Ezekiel looked off to the side and wiped his damp eyes.

Jon felt moved to do something that was out of character for him—he reached across the table and placed a hand on top of Ezekiel's.

Ezekiel continued: "My family abandoned me when I came out to them. I didn't want that for Tom. I didn't want him to lose his family the way I lost mine. So I did it; I played along with Tom's need to keep our life a secret from this family. I kept wishing that one day somebody in this family would break the ice, say they already knew who Tom really was, and then we could all be together, open and loving. It was a dream I had for him—for me."

"I know it is late, maybe too late, but is there anything I can do now?" Jon asked.

"I do want something. I want recognition. I know I say that sounding like it's just dawned on me today, but it didn't. Look," Ezekiel pulled at the knapsack again, "I've brought photos of our life together. I brought them to share. I think it would be nice for Elizabeth and Mrs. Hubbard to see how happy he was. You know, Jon, I said

I was looking for an ally, and I am. I'm telling you all this because you're the only one here today who seemed at all interested in who Tom was, who he really was."

Ezekiel turned to face Jon, looking him square in the eyes. "I want recognition for having loved Tom. Is that too much to ask?"

Jon sensed that Ezekiel had finished. "No, that's not too much. What would you like to do?"

As Jon waited for Ezekiel to respond, he considered the situation in the reception room. "Before you answer that, I do have one other question ..."

"Yes?"

Jon wanted to be sensitive to all the private sentiments that Ezekiel had shared, but instead he ended up sounding like an amateur detective. "Carrie Phillips and her son, what do you know about them?"

"I just met them today," Ezekiel answered cautiously; he had just confided in this man, and he asks this? *What does she have to do with me?* "She's friendly and the boy's a darling. Why do you ask?"

"You arrived together?"

Before Ezekiel could respond, Tony rushed into the kitchen from the access hallway frantically waving one hand in the air. Going straight for the sink, he pushed Gabriella aside and held his hand under cold running water. "Burned my hand, damn it. Goddamn log rolled out of the fireplace."

Tony's face was a mixture of apology and frustration. "¿Dónde está su ... what the heck ... Where's your grandson?" he asked, looking for someone to blame for his own stupidity—picking up a burning log, barehanded.

Patella went to the refrigerator. "¿Heilo, heilo? Ice, Ice?"

"You seen that kid, Marcos, Juan's son; he's been

taking care of the fires?" Tony asked, still shaking his hand for relief.

"No," Jon replied, annoyed by the interruption.

"No big deal," Tony said as Patella handed him ice wrapped in a dishtowel. "Gracias, thank you."

"By the way, Elizabeth asked if I'd seen you," Tony lied. He wanted Jon to leave so he could talk with Ezekiel alone. There was something that Aunt Casey, Patella and Gabriella had said about Tom that had bothered him ever since meeting Ezekiel earlier that afternoon.

"I'm sure she'll find me," Jon remarked curtly, trying to cut short the conversation with Tony.

Missing the gist of Jon's pointed reply, Tony leaned against the butcher-block counter and held the dishtowel with ice on his hand. "I'm Tony, Tom's cousin," he said to Ezekiel. "We met before, in there with my aunt," he nodded towards the sitting room with his chin.

"Yes, I remember," Ezekiel turned around to face Tony.

"I'm sorry we haven't had a chance to talk yet. My aunt was a little loopy from the whisky, but she said that you and Tom were partners—in the war. Or something like that?" Giving up on easing the pain of the burn, he dumped the ice into the sink, shook his hand again and wrapped the dishtowel around it.

"No," Ezekiel said with a nervous laugh. "That's not it at all." He turned to Jon, as if asking permission.

"You said you wanted recognition," Jon smiled.

And Ezekiel, looking relieved of a great burden, opened his arms wide and began to tell Tony everything.

Chapter Thirty-Three

Billy and Jeannine Quinn sat on the couch in the front parlor poking fun of Neil Bingham. Frustrated, Neil had repeatedly tried calling Ted Dorsey. Neil's plans were to catch a flight out of Boston's Logan Airport that night and he was nervous Ted had gone home and forgotten their arrangement.

"You'll be stuck in Newbury," Billy Quinn joked. "Now you'll have to move back to your hometown."

Neil rolled his eyes at Billy as Tony walked into the front parlor looking like he had just had the wind knocked out of him. Moments before, Ezekiel had told him that he and Tom had been partners. "We were as good as married," Ezekiel had said.

Ezekiel's frankness hit Tony hard. What he had wanted to hear instead was that his aunt, Gabriella and Patella had misunderstood Ezekiel earlier in the day, and that Tom and Ezekiel were merely close friends and not, as Ezekiel asserted, a homosexual couple. Struck dumb, Tony said nothing in reply to Ezekiel. He simply left the kitchen in a daze.

Now, in the front parlor, his face revealed a struggle to understand what Ezekiel had meant—*Did he mean that Tom and he just lived together? Or did he really mean they were ... homosexuals? Just the idea of it—*

"Tony?" Jeanine Quinn asked, concerned by his off-kilter expression. "Are you okay?" She pushed closer to her husband, freeing the seat on the couch next to her. "Here, sit down. Rest. You don't look good."

Tony stood in the center of the room, shoulders stooped over his heavy chest. He slid one hand into a pocket. The other hand still had the dishtowel wrapped loosely around it. "No thanks, Jeannine, I don't need to."

"You burned your hand grabbing that log, didn't you?" Billy asked.

"My hand? That's nothing."

Neil Bingham gave up trying to reach Ted Dorsey, snapped his phone shut and declared, "He probably just had to run home first. He'll be back." Ted was too reliable to blow him off. He leaned against the corner of a table and relaxed, turning his attention to Tony as well.

Tony wanted to blurt it all out, tell them all about Tom. But at the same time he wanted to protect them, have them continue to believe the great and honorable things they thought about Tom. Things he was sure they could never believe again once they lumped Tom into that stereotype of the queen, the flamer, the amoral fag—any of it. Honestly, he felt like crying—his third time today.

"Are you sure you're okay?" Jeannine grew more concerned. Her husband was just like this; she had to drag things out of him. For all she knew, Tony had burned that hand really badly and needed to go to the hospital.

"I guess so," Tony's voice betrayed him. One more push from Jeannine and he would tell them Tom was gay.

"Something's wrong, Tony." Jeannine was determined.

"Tony!" Elizabeth suddenly appeared in the living room doorway, hands on her hips. "Have you seen my husband?"

Tony turned slowly and looked at his cousin. "He's in the kitchen with that guy, Ezekiel." *She must have known Tom was gay,* he thought. *Why didn't they tell me? Do they think I'm that close-minded? Am I?*

"The kitchen?" Elizabeth repeated.

"Elizabeth?"

"What?"

"Why didn't you tell me?"

"Tell you what?" Elizabeth fired back at him, indignantly. She thought he'd heard about the child and wanted to head off any questions with harshness, to the tune of *None of your business!*

"Tell you what?" she impatiently repeated.

"That Tom was gay."

"What?"

Chapter Thirty-Three

By the time Julian and Melanie walked away from Tom's grave, Melanie had already slipped and fallen several times, muddying her pants and jacket. Then, as they made their way arm-in-arm down the cemetery slope to the car, she fell so hard she even pulled Julian down with her.

Besides wet pant legs and damp, chilly behind, she felt comfortable in a happy, drunken sort of way. Maintaining that mood, she snuggled next to Julian when he parked the car in the driveway. She had suggested they go to her house so she could change clothes before returning to the reception. Julian was only too happy to oblige, as he had hopes of breaking a three-year dry spell by sleeping with Melanie.

"Not much has changed in here," Julian commented as they entered Melanie's living room.

"No," Melanie agreed, looking for his approval.

The fact of the matter was that everything had changed in her house since she had sold the land across the street and stopped drinking. Five years ago, the last time he was over, the place was still furnished with the same junky tables, worn couches and tattered chairs she'd grown up with. After getting sober and selling the land, however, she replaced it all with new, modern, fancier-looking stuff. And the walls as well, over the past two years, received fresh coats of paint with warmer tones, the hardwood floors sanded and refinished.

"Make yourself comfortable," Melanie said, disappearing into the first floor bathroom.

"How about a drink?" Julian called out.

"You'll have to bring it in. I have nothing in the house," she shouted back.

Julian went out to the car and grabbed the plastic bottle of vodka stashed behind the driver's seat. Closing the door, he noticed the dark, skeletal frames of the two houses under construction across the street. Returning to the living room, he said, "I thought you owned the land across the street?"

"I'm in the kitchen," she shouted back, avoiding the topic of her land. She placed crackers on a plate. Two juice glasses waited for Julian to fill. "Want to mix that with anything?" she said, head down as he entered.

"Umm, I don't know. Do you?" He stopped in the center of the room, alarmed.

Melanie had changed into a pink, silky, thigh-length robe. She tied the matching belt so that the robe fit invitingly tight against her breasts, framing her cleavage.

She finished arranging the crackers. "There, that should do it," she smiled, looking up at him. "There's juice in the fridge, if you want to mix it." Carrying the plate into the living room, she sat on the couch. He picked up the two glasses and obediently followed.

Nervously, Julian sat next to her and poured straight vodka into the glasses. *Okay,* he thought, *we already made out. Don't blow it. She wants me.* Reaching an arm around her shoulders, allowing her to shift positions so she fit snug against his side, his penis filled with blood and began to throb. Turning, opening his mouth, he placed his lips around hers. Then pushing against her tongue with his, applying what he thought was the appropriate amount of pressure. Julian could feel her heavy, warm exhale brush against his cheeks as his hands fumbled with the knot of the robe.

Melanie really wanted to go upstairs, though she thought it appropriate to begin on the couch. She could feel from his kisses that he was nervous, even inexperienced. But the bulge in his pants proved his interest. She tried to remember five years ago. *Had I enjoyed it? Was he good?* Her memory of that night was gray. She had been drunk, too drunk to care.

Maybe they had both been too drunk to feel anything at all.

She felt his fingers pull on the knot. "Let's go up stairs," she said in a purposefully breathy voice. With his hand in hers, she led them to the bedroom on the second floor.

Julian stood silent and unsure at the foot of the bed. He wanted to be a man and lead. He wanted to be in control of the situation, his penis demanded it, but the rest of his body, awash in alcohol, was slow in responding.

Melanie saw his hesitation. So she let her robe fall open, unbuckled his pants and lifted off his shirt. He kicked off his shoes and socks and they fell together on the bed, wrapping their bodies around each other, pushing their mouths together and gasping for air. Melanie could feel herself getting wet as his hardness rubbed against her belly.

She took his penis in one hand and began to massage it. With her free hand she guided Julian's fingers down between her legs. She wanted him to caress her like she was caressing him. She wanted him to want to please her.

"Like this," she whispered, and placed his index finger directly on her hidden clitoris. Then she let go of his hand.

After a few uncomfortable seconds, Julian pulled his hand away from her crotch and moved it to her back. With his other, he roughly rubbed her breasts.

Frustrated with Julian's ineptitude, Melanie went for the next best alternative—she turned him onto his back and, climbing on top, positioned her opening over him. She held his cock in place as she lowered herself. She felt her vagina fill with his hardness.

Julian closed his eyes. He could feel her rise and fall, rise and fall. Letting his mind drift to his favorite porn site, he began to fantasize about the buxom brunette she-male he had been masturbating to this past week, starting when Melanie had called to tell him about Tom's death. He imagined that it was the she-male's mouth on him, not Melanie's body. Melanie's moans became the she-male's pleasure. The image shifted and now he envisioned his penis inside her ass, pounding harder, deeper.

Then the she-male turned on him, dominating him, forcing him to take her penis in his mouth and hold it there, fucking him and fucking him. Julian was close to coming and—his hard-on softened abruptly. The pornographic fantasy playing out in his head required a sensation far different from that of being inside Melanie. Besides, he'd grown dependent on the interaction between his hand, his penis and his computer screen—too dependent to orgasm with a real woman.

Feeling terribly empty, Melanie climbed off of Julian. Sitting up crossed-legged in bed, she pulled the sheets over her lap to cover herself.

"What?" Julian asked, his hard-on now completely gone. "What's wrong?"

"What's wrong?" she angrily repeated. "What's wrong? You're not here, that's what's wrong!"

Melanie climbed out of the bed and threw his pants at him. "No, you wanna know what's really wrong? I'm so fucking stupid, that's what's wrong!"

Embarrassed by his incompetence, Julian angrily pulled his pants on.

Even with all the drunken loneliness that Melanie had experienced in her life, having Julian's erection soften inside of her was by far the loneliest she had felt in a long time. And on top of that, she hated that she was drunk. "Two years sober, and I tossed it away on a loser like you."

Now, drunk or not, she wanted her family. Most especially she had to talk to her auntie and she had to talk to her now—*How did I let myself get so far away from them?*

"Hurry up," she yelled, rushing to get dressed. "Take me back to my aunt."

Chapter Thirty-Five

"**J**on, where the hell are you?" Elizabeth yelled from the living room. Her dumb-ass cousin Tony had just told her, the Quinns and Neil Bingham that her deceased war hero brother had been gay.

Tonight, not only has Tom been accused of abandoning a son, now he's a homosexual as well. She was furious and yelled again, "Jon!"

"Did you lose your husband, Lizzy?" Peter Hubbard sarcastically asked and then cocked his head to enlist his brother Alley's support. No one else was in the living room, just the old brothers sitting under the tall window.

"What of it?" she demanded.

"Nothin', nothin' at all," Peter Hubbard replied, tapping his hands on the wooden arms of the same chair he had sat in all day.

"I have no idea why you two jackasses are still here," Elizabeth muttered, stomping out of the quiet living room and back into the reception room where she once again met up with her mother, Carrie Phillips and the boy.

"Elizabeth," Mrs. Hubbard asked, "what's all that yelling about?"

Her attention was still on little Tommy who now

stood at her knees twisting the golden tassels on the fringe of the black shawl. "If you're looking for Jon, I think I heard him in the kitchen," she said flatly, encouraging Elizabeth to move along.

"Well, you all seem to be getting along famously," Elizabeth said sharply. She looked at Carrie Phillips who, sitting on the couch, hardly looked up at her when she walked into the room. *That woman thinks she's so clever, bringing the boy here to manipulate my gullible mother.* Elizabeth glared at Carrie. "Did you hear the latest about the boy's father?" Elizabeth seethed.

Carrie looked up, concern flashed across her face; her son was still blissfully ignorant as to his father.

Carrie wanted to first talk with the Hubbard family about how to tell the boy. But she had decided against rushing into that discussion; it was best to wait until they had accepted the idea that Tom had actually abandoned a child.

During the course of the evening, with events unfolding as they were, Carrie had concluded, almost immediately upon Elizabeth's negative reaction, that if the family were unwilling to accept her son then she would hold off on telling the boy about his father. After all, she needed to protect her son from any unnecessary emotional harm.

And, separately, she figured that at some point in the near future she would have to have yet another difficult conversation with the family, this time about the land. If it were indeed Tom's land, she would need to consider her son's financial future; there would be summer camps, music lessons, college tuition and many other expenses, opportunities that Tommy might otherwise miss because of her limited financial resources. The land could change all that.

Elizabeth responded to Carrie's look of concern with

a smug expression. "Well, there's now a rumor that Tom wasn't the man you claim him to be."

"Elizabeth!" her mother scolded. "I think I heard Jon talking to someone in the kitchen. Go see."

Like an upset child, Elizabeth stomped towards the door. As she did, one of her high-heeled shoes pinched the inside of her foot. The sharp pain made her want to cry out. She channeled the pain into a fiery hiss, "I can't believe you're buying into this crap, Mother," and slammed the door behind her.

On the kitchen table, Ezekiel had spread out all the photographs he had brought with him in the small knapsack. There were vacation photos from Puerto Rico and Costa Rica; shots of the two of them at friends' weddings, backyard barbeques and beach outings; and pictures of their house in Arlington, Virginia.

Standing out among the many pictures was a series of Christmas photos. Each featured Tom and Ezekiel in the same spot in their living room in Arlington, year after year, with a different decorated evergreen tree behind them. Ezekiel laughed as he pushed the other photos aside and placed the Christmas series in chronological order. Jon, Gabriella and Patella huddled around as Ezekiel spoke about the evolution of the precariously placed self-timer cameras.

Over the years, Ezekiel explained, their strategy of picture-taking changed from simply tilting up the angle of the camera with a couple of quarters on the arm of their couch, to placing the camera on an elaborate makeshift tower Tom fashioned together out of a foot stool, an upside down trash bin and two thick picture books. The older photos featured cut-off foreheads and half-faces, while the most recent ones rivaled any photo taken with a well-placed tripod.

"Tom called tripods 'unnecessary, fancy-schmancy' equipment. He insisted we didn't need one. And he was right, because he could build anything out of nothing," Ezekiel laughed again.

"He was so proud of this last one," Ezekiel passed the picture to Gabriella.

"Bonito," Gabriella said. Though she did not understand his explanation, she heard the affection in Ezekiel's voice. She held it for Patella who smiled in agreement.

"And this one, it's just our noses." Ezekiel touched the photo and the four of them laughed together.

Jon moved the images around on the table. There was his brother-in-law, a clean-cut, sturdy, blonde man. He could see very little of his dark haired wife in Tom's features—just the eyes mostly. Tom had the same steady, warm, but protected gaze as Elizabeth. Even with a broad smile, his eyes looked as though they had a story to tell, but chose to hold back instead—just like Elizabeth's eyes.

Jon picked up a photograph and studied it. There was Ezekiel, taller and bigger than Tom, smiling in his colorful Hawaiian shirt, hands resting on Tom's shoulders. And there was a tanned Tom, smiling with the same cheekbones, balled jaw and square chin that he had passed along to the boy in the next room. And for the first time since Elizabeth had told Jon about Tom's death, he felt as though he had actually lost something. He looked around the kitchen, half-expecting to see Tom there by the sink, at the refrigerator, coming in the back door. Jon felt the back of his throat tug the way it had when his first child was born.

Gabriella placed a hand on Jon's back to offer support. She knew more about death from war than most and she could see Jon was feeling Tom's absence.

Ezekiel took Jon's hand. They sat together, Jon, Ezekiel, Patella and Gabriella, in respectful silence with the photos spread in front of them on the kitchen table. Jon's mind finally cleared—unlike earlier, during the burial's moment of silence, when his mind had wandered, unfocused. Then, instead of praying or grieving, he had found himself scanning the crowd, guessing each mourner's relationship to Tom. At last, with this small group at the kitchen table, Jon finally let the loss of his brother-in-law wash over him.

"For Christ's sake, Jon, here you are." Elizabeth stepped into the kitchen, slamming the door to the small sitting room behind her. "Do you know what's going on in that room? That little wench is using her boy to manipulate my mother!"

Jon quickly composed himself and the temporarily bonded foursome separated.

Elizabeth positioned herself at the head of the table, oblivious to the quiet grieving she had just interrupted. The tendons in her neck flexed.

"Oh," she said, snapping back into the role of domineering hostess. She reached across the table towards Ezekiel—"Elizabeth, Tom's sister. I don't think we've met."

"No, not really." Ezekiel shook her hand. "At least not in person."

"I'm sorry," Elizabeth mockingly apologized, interpreting the comment to mean she was rude for not having introduced herself sooner. "With the number of guests here today, I couldn't break away and meet everyone. I apologize for missing you."

Gabriella and Patella heard the strain in Elizabeth's voice, like that of a spoiled child, and moved to the dining room to busy themselves.

"I imagine the day has been stressful for you," Ezekiel spoke softly, agreeing with Elizabeth. "My name is Ezekiel."

"Yes, it is," she replied, attention shifting to the array of photographs on the table.

Jon moved around the table next to her. After seven years of marriage, he had learned when it was best to give Elizabeth a chance to catch her breath. And then, sometimes, like perhaps now, there would be a rare opening, a crack in her armor, when he could intercept her anger and steer it off course, disarming her with his quiet affection. He stood near Elizabeth and took her hand.

Using one finger Elizabeth dragged a single photograph across the table and then spun it around so it faced her. It was of Ezekiel and Tom, arm in arm, holding a "sold" sign on the front lawn of a small house. She remained silent as she reached across the table for another. Then she reached for another and another, slowly moving the photographs around the table until the bulk of them lay in front of her.

Jon waited, prepared for whichever reaction Elizabeth might have—denial, dismissal, anger, acceptance, or even love. Jon was ready for her tears—and if not tears, he was semi-confident he could handle her anger.

Ezekiel just hoped for the best.

Chapter Thirty-Six

Elizabeth held an eight by ten, black and white photograph of Tom as a boy with the farmhouse behind. "This is what I told you about, Jon, what I remember. See, it was just like this—like growing up someplace else, in another era." Elizabeth bit the inside of her lip. "Look at him, he was just a boy!" For her, Tom had never lived a life outside of Newbury. Apart from her memories of their time growing up on the farm, she never actually considered that her older brother Tom had had a life of his own, a life beyond their childhood.

Jon, standing next to her, looked at the black and white photo. There he was, Tom as a boy of not more than five years old, the farmhouse and farmland. But it could have easily been a picture of the little boy in the next room. "Was that taken right here, out front?"

"Yes, it was," she said, and then looked toward Ezekiel who had stepped out of the way to give her plenty of room while she sifted through his pile of photographs.

"He gave all these to you?" she asked, ignoring Ezekiel's presence in the pictures.

"That one you're holding was Tom's favorite," Ezekiel said. "I have a framed print of it in our bedroom. You're welcome to that one, if you'd like."

Elizabeth blinked: *Was this man for real? Offering me a photograph of my brother and our farm? Who the hell does he think he is?*

"What are you saying? That you have a photograph of our farm in your bedroom?"

"Elizabeth," Jon tried to intervene as he heard his wife's voice begin to twist with tension.

"Hush, Jon. I want to understand what this man is saying."

"He's not saying anything other than the fact that he and your brother, Tom and him, lived a full life together."

"Well, that's his business. But this is my business." She shook the eight by ten by its corner. "This is my life that he has hanging on his wall and I just want to know why he thinks he has the right to come here and—"

Elizabeth stopped; evidence of her brother's life as a gay man was there, spread out on the table in front of her. She wanted to deny it more than anything, but the photographs disarmed her.

"—come here and—and tell us how my brother lived his life. Bullshit! That's what I say. Bullshit!"

"Please, that wasn't my intention at all. I didn't—" Ezekiel heard anger and saw disgust in Elizabeth's face and posture.

"Tell me then, tell me all about it. What are you trying to say? My brother was a faggot? Is that it?" She circled the table and picked up a photo from Ezekiel and Tom's Christmas series. The picture cut off Ezekiel's head and one of Tom's arms. She held up the photograph and demanded, "How old is this picture? Tell me, how old is this picture?"

"That was our first Christmas together—in our house."

"How old is the picture?"

"Elizabeth ..." Jon tried to stop her.

"What are you afraid of?" she snapped at him.

Jon backed down.

Turning to Ezekiel she yelled, "Just answer the damn question! How long ago was this photo taken?"

"Eight years."

"Eight years, he says, 'Eight years.' And you were together the whole time? Since this photo?"

"We were together for ten years total."

"Ten years? Bullshit," Elizabeth yelled again. "And you know how I know? Do you want to know how I know? I know because there's a woman in the other room right now manipulating my mother with a boy she claims is Tom's. Can you believe it? And the fucking child is five years old. So are you telling me my gay brother was busy making babies with a straight woman while you and he had set up a happy gay home? Is that it?"

Ezekiel's mouth dropped open, the names popped into his head, *Carrie and Tommy? Of course, of course.* The kitchen shrunk around him, confining him. The light seemed to vibrate, getting brighter then dimmer. His ears hummed. He felt weak.

Elizabeth knew she had hit him hard. She wanted him to react, retaliate just as forcefully. She wanted him to get mad at her, to defend himself, to yell loudly, to argue bitterly. Instead, he quietly pulled a chair to the table and sat down. He needed time to let Elizabeth's accusations sink in.

Elizabeth glared at Jon. She wanted Jon to say something, anything, reprimand her for being so brutal toward Ezekiel. If he did, she would yell even louder. She wanted to scream until someone could explain to her how her brother's life had become so fucked up.

Earlier that day, as the trumpet player blew taps and her brother's casket was lowered into the ground, she was free to remember Tom as she had imagined him. She had believed that her brother lived a simple and private life. He had been a man who remained in contact with his family, sending annual Christmas/Chanukah cards and birthday gifts, and if he could have he would have spent more time with them. He had been a man of honor and duty who had the misfortune of giving his life for what she considered a useless and misguided war. In reality, Tom had been all those things, in one form or another, just not in the way she had wanted.

Elizabeth had nowhere left to turn and no one left to argue with. It was true, she only knew her brother as a child.

Elizabeth's angry voice penetrated the quiet of the reception room, upsetting Tommy and prompting Carrie Phillips to suggest to Mrs. Hubbard that they move their small party a bit further away, into the living room. Once there, however, Carrie found that if she listened closely she could still hear snippets of what sounded like Elizabeth interrogating Ezekiel.

Curious as to why Elizabeth was venting on him, she made the excuse that she had lost something, a bracelet, on the reception room couch. She left Tommy with Mrs. Hubbard and returned to the small room alone to eavesdrop.

Carrie heard Elizabeth question Ezekiel about a photograph, and she heard his reply—"It was eight years ago." Carrie strained to listen in; she wanted to hear if the ruckus Elizabeth was making had anything to do with her or her son.

"Bullshit!" Elizabeth's voice filtered through, and then she said something that had never entered Carrie's mind as a reason why Tom had behaved the way he had toward her. Apparently, when she was having her fling with Tom, when she had become pregnant, Tom had been cheating on his boyfriend, Ezekiel. She sat on the couch and stared at the fire roaring away in the fireplace. Tom had been gay.

The kitchen fell silent. Then Carrie heard the doorknob rattle and jumped up to fulfill the promise of her original excuse. She rummaged around the pillows of the couch as if having dropped something. The door opened and Elizabeth and Jon stepped into the room.

"Lose something?" Jon asked.

"Oh, nothing really, just a bracelet. It could be anywhere. I just looked at my wrist and realized I'd lost it." Carrie Phillips stood and straightened her long skirt, continuing to scan the floor and couch with a made-up perplexed expression.

"Do you need a hand?" Jon began to look around the floor for the non-existent bracelet.

"No, that's fine. It was more sentimental than anything," Carrie replied, pursing her lips. Looking at the two of them, Carrie noticed that Elizabeth appeared exhausted, resigned. The anger that had seemed to drip off her the last time she had passed through the small sitting room was now gone, drained away.

Elizabeth's eyes rested on her mother's empty chair. "Where did my mother go?"

"My son's entertaining her in the living room."

"Should we join them?" Elizabeth weakly asked Jon and motioned to the door.

"You'll join us, too?" Jon invited Carrie as they exited to the living room.

Carrie nodded and returned to looking for a non-existent bracelet. Then, satisfied that Elizabeth and Jon had joined Mrs. Hubbard and her son, she slid into the kitchen to find Ezekiel.

Chapter Thirty-Seven

After entering the kitchen, Carrie pulled the door closed and hovered by the wall waiting for Ezekiel to look up from the photographs of Tom and acknowledge her. She could tell by his pensive expression that he was digesting the just disclosed news that Tom was her son's father.

Deep in thought, Ezekiel rearranged the photographs on the table. At first, Elizabeth's news that Tom had fathered a child clobbered him like a wave, catching him off guard and tossing him off balance to the point that he needed to sit down before he fell down. Now that Ezekiel thought about the boy's age, close to five, it made sense. That coincided with a rocky period when he and Tom had argued almost constantly about seemingly needless things, like folding laundry and washing dishes and who was seeing whom. He recalled that Tom had become so unhappy he temporarily moved out, claiming to need time to evaluate their relationship.

After that difficult period, however, when Tom moved back in, Ezekiel remembered that they entered what he thought of as the happiest phase of their relationship. *We had matured.* In Ezekiel's mind, that short separation had also introduced a new depth of trust between them. He thought that many of the obstacles, the little nit-picks that had kept them arguing, had fallen away. But, Ezekiel was now discovering, in reality his trust had been misplaced, for it was during that rocky period, when they had separated, before they had gotten back together, when Tom fathered a child and kept it a secret from him. Ezekiel had always been keenly aware of Tom's interest in women, his bisexuality. He even knew that at times, especially early on in their relationship, Tom had had affairs with women. They talked about it. And when they talked about having children of their own, they discussed using a surrogate mother, and if the mother agreed, Tom wanted to do the deed himself, actively partaking in the making of their baby.

Damn it, why didn't I notice it myself; the boy even looks like him. Ezekiel looked up and saw Carrie standing by the doorway. His face displayed a need to talk.

Carrie spoke as she approached, "I overheard Elizabeth."

She sat down, the photos spread on the table between them. Her tone was open and friendly; she wanted to be respectful of the pain he was feeling.

"Well, actually, I have to admit, I was eavesdropping in the other room. I thought you and Elizabeth were talking about Tommy and me."

"So you know it all then? Well, I don't," Ezekiel spoke quickly, almost curtly. "There is one thing: Did Tom know he was the father?"

"Yes," she answered cautiously, though she suspected that Ezekiel would refrain from reacting with the same animosity Elizabeth had.

"Why didn't you tell me he was Tom's son?"

Carrie, tired of having to explain her actions, spoke softly. "I didn't know you even existed until earlier today, and I had no idea that you were Tom's lover until a few moments ago. I haven't spoken to or seen Tom since just after Tommy's birth."

Her patience stretched, her soft demeanor turned defensive. "Besides how was I to know he had a lover? Least of all, a lover who was a man."

She had done nothing wrong. She had chosen to raise the boy on her own. Tom chose to return to Ezekiel. How could she have known that Tom had a relationship with him while he was with her? In her mind, Tom had betrayed them both.

"I was more than his lover," he corrected her. "I was his partner. We were together for ten years."

"Partner, yes, you were his partner." Carrie watched Ezekiel's sad, disillusioned eyes scan over the photos. She breathed slowly, meditatively. She could feel his loss. After all, Tom had left her, too, years before. She, however, still had Tommy.

A kitchen clock ticked loudly as they sat in silence.

"You had a life together," Carrie said at length. "Look at all these beautiful photos."

"Yes," Ezekiel responded quietly, thoughtfully agreeing. He liked Carrie. He felt comfortable with her near him. Although he had only met her that day, he thought he understood Tom's attraction to her, as a person. "I've been sitting here thinking ... It's funny how much your son looks like Tom. I didn't notice the resemblance at first ... when we met outside in the street." His voice perked up, "I only thought, 'Well, isn't little Tommy such a handsome boy.'"

"A very handsome boy, a little gentleman. He reminds me of his father." She placed both elbows onto the table and dropped her chin into her palm. She looked at Ezekiel with big blue eyes that displayed a willingness to listen.

Ezekiel held up a photograph of Tom. "I want to get

angry at the past, at Tom."

"For cheating?"

"Yes, for cheating." He placed the photo down and, looking squarely at Carrie, continued: "We had times when everything between us wasn't so perfect. I'm not a saint either, or for that matter even a practicing Christian," he chuckled. "But it hurts. It hurts. I end up questioning what Tom and I had, and who Tom was. And I don't want to do that."

He paused and swallowed hard.

"Tom and I, we had our difficult times. Yet, I loved him and still love him and that's all that matters."

Searching Carrie's eyes, Ezekiel saw that part of her still loved Tom, too.

"He never mentioned anything to you?" Carrie whispered, embarrassed but curious. Yes, Tom had broken her heart. She blushed slightly. She, like Ezekiel, wanted recognition for having once loved the man.

"Not a word," Ezekiel said compassionately. "I don't know how he managed to keep you and Tommy such a secret. I'm stunned. Tom could be such a blabber mouth."

"He *was* a blabber mouth, wasn't he?"

They laughed.

Ezekiel reached across the table and picked up the black and white photograph of Tom as a boy with the farmhouse behind him. "This was his favorite. Look, do you see your little Tommy there, in Tom's face?"

"How absolutely adorable. They could be twins." Carrie's face glowed looking at the photo. Then she lowered her voice and said, "You know, I've told him very little about his father. Maybe it's because of his peers. They're mostly single-parent children, too. Hell, he doesn't even know that his father is dead, or who any of these people are. Then again, he doesn't ask me about any of that, anyway. Not yet." She paused and added, "I worry what he thinks sometimes. Although he talks a lot, he doesn't ask many questions for a boy his age. Sometimes I think he's trying to protect me."

"He takes after his father."

"I would love to have some of these to show Tommy," Carrie said, picking up another photo, "to help him get to know this place, his father's history, all of it, Tom's mother—and you. I want him to know you."

Ezekiel's heart leapt like he had just received the most perfect gift.

Carrie looked around the kitchen and waved her arms: "So he has something. Do you understand? Some roots, some history, something to hold onto."

Chapter Thirty-Eight

The darkened windows, the roaring fire in the stone hearth and the table and floor lamps with their Victorian shades all gave the large living room a golden glow. Gabriella and Patella wandered about wiping up drink rings and collecting paper plates from the odd places the guests had stashed them after they had finished eating. Elizabeth, Jon and Mrs. Hubbard were gathered on the couch and stuffed armchairs at the end of the room by the fireplace watching little Tommy roll a drink caster around the coffee table like it was the wheel of a toy car. Peter and Alley Hubbard watched the boy play as well. Occasionally they would perk up and take note of what was being said, but most of the time they appeared to be drunkenly drifting off.

Elizabeth kicked off her shoes and crossed her legs. "How nice of you two to join us," she snipped at Carrie and Ezekiel as they entered the room. She twisted her back on the cushions of the stuffed chair in search of a more comfortable position.

"Here," Jon said, slidding over on the couch, inviting the newcomers to join them.

Mrs. Hubbard smiled fondly at each. Although her eyes remained on the boy, her thoughts were focused on what Jon and Elizabeth had told her about Tom's relationship with Ezekiel. Her son had been gay, they said, and then they did their best to minimize the true nature of Tom and Ezekiel's relationship by avoiding amorous and explicate terms, like *lovers*.

Kind of them to try to protect me, she thought. But in truth, she was happy. *Though I buried a son today, I gained a grandson and his beautiful mother, and I also get...* There was the difficulty defining Ezekiel, *this other man who loved my son. I get him, too.* She had an overwhelming desire to express gratitude and love towards each and every person in the room. But a lifetime of burying emotions safely inside prevented her from doing so.

Mrs. Hubbard glanced up and caught Patella's sympathetic eye. *My new friends are so helpful*, she thought, unaware Elizabeth paid them to clean. "Leave that," she said, motioning to both her and Gabriella. "Sit, sit. Please join us."

Elizabeth shook her head in disapproval, "No."

So Gabriella and Patella remained on the fringe of the family circle offering Mrs. Hubbard a polite, "No gracias."

As if just waking from a catnap, the two old Hubbard brothers grunted and stirred, looking for attention. They had listened in on Jon and Elizabeth's talk with Mrs. Hubbard and were up-to-date on the status of Carrie Phillips, the boy and Ezekiel. Now everyone in the Hubbard family knew everything.

"How's my little man?" Carrie asked as Tommy embraced one leg through her long skirt.

"Sit," Elizabeth said to Ezekiel, motioning toward a chair and offering an artificial smile. "It's been along day."

"Thank you."

Nervous, Ezekiel realized that for the first time he was sitting down with Tom's whole family. For him, this constituted the initial step in building a face-to-face connection with them—a big and positive move beyond the anonymous relationship he had painstakingly maintained for Tom's sake.

Jon winked reassuringly at Ezekiel. He recognized the man's nervousness having experienced it himself, before his wedding, when first met Elizabeth's family.

"Shhhh," Elizabeth reprimanded her husband for the wink. Then, pointing to a spot on the couch next to Jon, she suggested that Carrie, "Join the family."

Elizabeth resigned herself to the fact that her brother had, by all appearances, fathered the boy, and that Ezekiel was indeed her brother's partner. She was unhappy about it and entertained very little intention of ever being happy about it, but she would tolerate them, which meant that she would accept them all—the boy, his mother and her brother's gay lover—on her terms. She would welcome them, but only with a forced smile and the appearance of kindness.

"Thanks, Elizabeth, but I think I'll stand for a bit. I feel like I've been sitting all day," Carrie said, brushing her son's hair with her hand. They had stayed longer and became much more involved with Tom's family than she had ever intended.

Tommy was comfortable with them. However, she needed to plan for their departure, wanting their leaving to go smoothly, without drama; a few well-placed words about future plans, then out to the car.

"Carrie, I think you have as much energy and spunk as that boy," Mrs. Hubbard gushed, complimenting her.

"Oh, I don't know about my spunk or energy," she said, seeing an out, a way to turn the conversation toward her imminent departure. "He is certainly a challenge to keep up with. I think the day is beginning to wear on him, though. I imagine he'll sleep well on the ride home."

Tommy held onto Carrie's hand and spun around so he faced the family. He leaned back against his mother's leg and let his head droop.

"Let me just say this ..." Slurring words as he prepared to give Carrie advice on the topic of spunk and energy, old Peter Hubbard pushed his way into the conversation.

"Oh, Jesus, here we go," Elizabeth sighed disdainfully.

"Look here, missy—" Peter Hubbard shifted in his seat and pointed his pipe stem at Elizabeth. "Seems to me your mother forgot to teach you about respecting your elders, but that's not the point I'm tryin' to make here."

He turned back to Carrie.

Elizabeth's comment had thrown him off track. But not for long. Peter began to drunkenly philosophize. "You see, spunk only lasts so long and then other things ... complications, take it away." This profound statement met with silence, so he tried again: "What I'm saying is that when you get older and things slow down, things that didn't mean so much then begin to take on more meaning. Like Tom's life, for example, and this war. Think. There was Tom living his life and then this war came, see?"

Elizabeth, fed up with the day's events, challenged her uncle. "Just what the fuck do you know about Tom's life?" She impatiently tapped a foot. "Isn't it time for you two to put the stopper in the bottle, pack it up and head home?"

"Elizabeth, he's just talking. Excuse her, it's been a tough day." Jon immediately wished he had chosen to swallow his words instead. If he had remained quiet there was a chance, just a chance, that his wife, after her last comment, might have dropped the conversation. His remark, however, only fueled Elizabeth's temper.

"You butt out," she pointed at Jon and then glared at the Hubbard brothers.

Elizabeth wanted a fight. She had accepted the boy, his mother and Tom's gay lover, but these two, along with their brother, her dead father, represented all of the reasons why she thought her own brother had behaved the way he had. Became gay the way he became gay. Abandoned his child the way he abandoned his child. Avoided visiting his family the way he avoided visiting his family. And, eventually, got killed in a senseless war. To her, these two curmudgeons were siphons. Like her father, they had sucked the life out of Tom's youth, and now she was sure they intended to sink their teeth into the last thing that at was still Tom's.

"Elizabeth," her mother sharply cautioned, "for the sake of your brother, God rest his soul, remain civil."

"Are you serious, Mother? These two old bastards have been hanging around here like vultures. All day they've waited to swoop down and grab the last scraps of Tom's life—his land—and we all know it!"

"Elizabeth, this is not the time or the place," Mrs. Hubbard warned.

"Vultures, Mother, vultures waiting to pick apart the last of the farm." Then Elizabeth turned on Carrie and Ezekiel. "Do you two want to be part of this family? Is that it? Do you think you have a claim on Tom's land, too?"

"Elizabeth," Jon interjected. "Your mother is right; this is not the time or place."

Ignoring her husband, Elizabeth continued, "Do you? Well, Carrie? Ezekiel? No disrespect, but if you believe you have a claim on that part of Tom's life, then you should jump in right now and defend yourselves, because these two old bastards will most likely drag us all into court again over that land. Am I right?"

She practically spit on the living room rug as she wagged a finger at them.

"Uhh," Ezekiel was at a loss for both thoughts and words.

Ally Hubbard erupted with a drunken slur, "Now listen here, little girl, your mother made her choice a long time ago. And that choice had consequences."

Carrie pulled Tommy close to protect him.

"That's enough," Mrs. Hubbard slapped her knee.

"Casey, aren't you ever going to tell this girl the truth about her brother?" Peter Hubbard leaned forward to see the old woman's reaction as he challenged her.

"That's enough! I won't have you dragging this out today." Reeling from the tension and anger that now seemed to emit from every corner of the old farmhouse's living room, Mrs. Hubbard began to shake.

"After all these years, and he's dead now," Peter Hubbard forged ahead. "Don't you think it's about time to give our brother his rightful dignity? He deserves it, for Christ's sake. Tell us who the bastard's father was."

Mrs. Hubbard crossed her arms over her chest and shook in distress.

Ezekiel sprung from his chair and pulled the shawl around her as she rattled in her seat.

Carrie slipped out of the room and into the parlor with Tommy. The argument was incomprehensible to her. The outburst, the language, the violence vibrating in the air frightened her and Tommy. Never had she subjected the boy to anything resembling this.

Jon stood up, too. He wanted to defend someone, but was unsure who needed his help.

"Opened a can of worms, didn't you, missy," Alley Hubbard stated coolly from his chair.

Tony passed Carrie and Tommy on his way into the living room from the front parlor. He had heard the argument and assumed the brothers had instigated it. Now, positioning himself across from the old men, he prepared to remove them from the house if necessary.

Alley Hubbard sized Tony, now standing in front of him, up and down. "What are you gonna do, defend your bastard cousin's honor? Come on, Mr. Griffin, we both know your father, like us, knew the truth. Hell, we even know you were there that day when it was explained to Tom himself."

"I won't stand for this," Jon angrily declared.

"What are you gonna do?" Peter Hubbard laughed. "This is a family matter. It has nothing to do with you."

Defeated, Jon sat down. Ezekiel, however, remained standing. He had no idea what everyone was talking about. *Was there a question about Tom's father? Tom had never mentioned anything about that, or about land. Did Tom own land?*

The argument lulled. Tommy could be heard crying in the parlor with his mother attempting to calm him down. The Quinns, also in the parlor, were preparing to leave, and Neil Bingham had gone outside to the portico to wait for Ted Dorsey to return and pick him up. Gabriella, Patella and Eduardo were in the kitchen preparing to leave as well.

Elizabeth, who had started the argument, now stared blankly at the floor. She remembered the rumors that had circulated around town when she was a child about who Tom's father actually was. Like everyone else, she thought the rumors had finally disappeared because there was no basis to them.

"Wait." Confused, seeking clarity, Ezekiel prepared

to ask a question. "Are you saying that Tom's father ..." He didn't know what to ask, this was all new to him.

"Go ahead, ask. Why not? We heard you had a bit of Tom's ass yourself. And we're guessing, that—" Alley Hubbard stopped, twisted his mustache and turned to his brother for confirmation.

"Uh-huh," Peter Hubbard nodded, cocksure, leaning back in his chair.

"We're guessing that you're here to claim your share of Tom's land, too," Alley Hubbard said, pushing out his lips. "Just like that boy in there, weeping away, is gonna do. Or at least his mother will. She probably thinks her son has as much a rightful claim to this property as his father did—son of a whore that he was."

"That's ri—"

Before Peter Hubbard could finish, Ezekiel lifted his brother Ally up by the shirt collar and headed toward the front door, dangling the old man like a Raggedy Ann doll.

"Jesus Christ, you big homo asshole! Let my brother go." Peter sprang to his feet, then lost his balance, staggered, tripped and fell to the floor.

Taking a cue from Ezekiel, Tony bent down and caught Peter Hubbard by his belt and the back of his shirt and lifted the old man as if lifting a baby cradle. Tony headed toward the front door when all of a sudden a faint boom was heard in the distance.

The floorboards quaked.

Everyone fell silent.

"What was that?" Elizabeth asked, looking around the room.

It had begun faintly, in the background, a low thumping sound—only nobody had noticed it during the family commotion. Now, the thud-like noises grew louder and came at regular intervals until they reverberated through the building like an approaching freight train.

The old farmhouse began to rumble.

Chapter Thirty-Eight

It started to pour almost as soon as Melanie and Julian left her house. The drive back to the Hubbard farmhouse had been tense and silent.

"What's that?" Melanie strained forward to see through the furious swipes of the windshield wipers.

An orange hazy light jumped in the mist just above the tree line at the end of Hay Street.

"Probably nothing," Julian dismissed her. Too drunk to keep both eyes open, he drove with one eye closed and squinted through the lid of the other. He tried to concentrate on following the centerline of the road, yet he couldn't keep the car from swinging too wide around the bend.

Melanie glowered at him. She considered his dismissive tone and sloppy driving an undeserving attack resulting from their unsuccessful sexual romp. But she decided that his irritation was his problem—he'd been the one who'd let *her* down.

Julian, however, was more concerned about his blood-alcohol level and the upcoming thirty-five mile drive from the Hubbard's back to his apartment than he was about what he considered to be Melanie's resentful attitude toward him after her pushiness in bed.

Julian accelerated past the last stretch of trees that ran along Hay Street. He allowed the car to drift to the right before snapping the wheel sharply left, spinning the car onto Quinns Way.

"Holy shit!" Melanie exclaimed.

In the distance, the top of the chimney at the Hubbard farmhouse was ablaze. Like a roman candle, the chimney appeared to first breathe in and then push out a ball of fire with a boom.

"Oh my God. Where's my phone—" Melanie searched her jacket pockets as fire continued to exhale from the chimney. She had left her phone at her house. "Shit, gimmie your fucking phone."

"I don't have one, I don't have one—" Reaching anxiously into the back seat with one hand, Julian checked that his half-gallon bottle of vodka was properly hidden. Even though there were no flashing lights, he feared the police were already there.

"Shit! Drive, drive!" Adrenaline mixed with the alcohol in Melanie's brain and, thinking Julian's reflexes too slow, she grasped the steering wheel. The car jerked back and forth between the bounds of the road.

Julian pushed her away and retrieved the wheel.

Horrified with her inability to do anything but watch, Melanie stuck her head out of the passenger side window and yelled into the pouring rain.

"Auntie, I'm coming! I'm coming!"

Chapter Forty

Besides being exhausted, Neil Bingham was uncomfortable. Within one hour, the image he had held of his old friend Tom went from that of a track-star-turned-courageous-patriot to that of a queer guy who abandoned his son. So when Carrie Phillips ushered her (and apparently Tom's) son Tommy into the front parlor to escape the argument in the living room, Neil felt even more awkward. He excused himself from a conversation with Billy and Jeannine Quinn and stepped outside to wait for Ted Dorsey to pick him up.

Protected from a dousing rain by the portico, Neil lit a cigarette. After tossing the match, he looked up and noticed strange bursts of orange and yellow light, like an apparition, reflecting off the trees across the street. Curious as to the cause of the mystical flashes, he stepped into the rain and peered up at the farmhouse's roof. Flames spouted from the chimney. Agog, Neil rushed toward the front door just in time for Ezekiel, dangling old Alley Hubbard by the shirt collar, to plow into him. Neil tumbled back out the door. Tony came next, dragging Peter Hubbard behind.

Considering the arguments he'd overheard, Neil guessed that the Hubbard brothers' removal was the result of something other than the chimney flames. So he ran in yelling, "Fire! Fire! Everybody out! Evacuate!"

Trusting Neil's alarm, Jeannine Quinn immediately called 911 on her cell phone. She pulled a coat on and spoke to the emergency operator as she headed out the front door.

Without thinking, Carrie Phillips picked up Tommy and, following closely behind Jeannine, carried him outside.

Neil pointed to the living room; Billy Quinn accepted his directions and went to alert the others. Neil headed toward the dining room and the kitchen.

In the living room, Jon and Elizabeth were pulling a stubborn Mrs. Hubbard by the arms. The old woman rejected the calls of alarm and refused to budge and abandon her house. She dug her feet into the floor, her fingers into the cushioned armrests, and fought to keep her position on the couch. Billy Quinn entered the room and, ignoring any discussion, pleas or resistance the old woman had, wrapped his big arms around her tiny waist. In what seemed like one effortless move, he lifted her up over his shoulder and carried her through the living room, the parlor and out the front door to the driveway. Running, Jon and Elizabeth followed after him.

Patella and Eduardo remained calm. Having cleaned the house the day before, they were familiar with Mrs. Hubbard's abundant belongings. So, thinking clearly, they went to a closet at the end of the entrance hall and grabbed all the coats and umbrellas they could carry.

Neil, still trying to evacuate the house, passed through the dining room and access hallway. Empty. But in the kitchen he found Gabriella. She was piling Ezekiel's photographs into his small knapsack. Neil, thinking she misunderstood the urgency of the fire, grabbed her by the arm—"Leave it!"

She pushed him away with, "Importante," and then zipped the knapsack, swung it over her shoulder and swiftly exited the house through the cluttered kitchen back doorway.

Satisfied she was safely outside, Neil pushed forward, circling through the reception room, living room and out the parlor. In the entrance hallway a thick cloud of smoke began to roll down the stairs from the second floor. The loud thuds and booms that had originally been intermittent now sounded like a roaring crowd. Neil ran out into the driveway, panting, struggling to breath.

It had been the layers of thick, hard creosote, dangerously built up inside the 200-year-old chimney, which had finally caught fire. The roof, once exposed to the flame, smoldered like a pile of damp kindling, billowing clouds of smoke until it suddenly went up in a clean rush of fire. Uncontained, the fire spread. In a flash, the whole roof was aflame.

About halfway down the driveway, a safe distance from the house, Jon, Elizabeth and her mother huddled under two umbrellas. Carrie and Tommy stood under the musty coat Ezekiel draped over their heads and held up like a tent with his arms. Jeannine and Billy Quinn pulled their coats tight and shared an umbrella. Gabriella, Patella and Eduardo huddled together for a minute under one umbrella. Then, Gabriella returned the knapsack to Ezekiel and she, Patella and Eduardo, afraid of the police due to their undocumented status, slipped off together, undetected, into the night. The old Hubbard brothers stood off to the side and covered their heads with the red windbreaker jacket Eduardo had handed them as he left.

They all gawked like an awe-struck crowd at a pep-rally bonfire. Although the farmhouse burned in front of them, none could quite comprehend what was happening or why they had assembled outside the way they had.

Tony stood closest to the burning house. Without cover, the rain soaked him while he supplied the Captain of Newbury's Volunteer Fire Department with an account of the fire on his cell phone. "The second floor is burning now, too! Yes, the place is empty. Everyone's out," Tony said as Neil's black silhouette emerged from the darkened portico.

Carrying an open umbrella, Jon rushed passed Tony toward Neil. "You're fucking crazy, going through the house like that. What were you thinking? Here—" He tilted his umbrella over Neil.

"Is everyone out?" Tony shouted, questioning the validity of what he had just told the Fire Chief.

"I checked the first floor—it's empty." Neil looked over his shoulder at the burning farmhouse and trembled with disbelief at his own heroics.

In a lower, more cautious voice, Tony updated the Fire Chief: "He's the last one ... I think—"

Jon patted Neil on the back, complimenting him on his daring deed or lucky stupidity. "Shit, I can't believe you stayed in there. You actually checked all the rooms?"

Using the cover of the umbrella, Jon guided Neil to Tony. Positioning the umbrella in the middle, he shielded their heads. A steady stream of rain ran off the umbrella and soaked their backs. "What did they say?" Jon asked.

"They're on their way." As Tony spoke, thin whining sirens rose in the blackness beyond the orange orb of the flames. The sound of help coming emerged from several directions. "Any minute now," he managed to say between heavy breaths. "I think we're really lucky ... damn."

Ezekiel saw the flames of the roof reflect in Mrs. Hubbard's wet eyes. Although unable to see the old woman's individual features, hidden as they were by Elizabeth's shadow, from what he could see her expression plainly displayed complete devastation. Ezekiel wanted to hold her, to stand with her and offer support. Another new responsibility, however, kept him from going to her. Carrie and Tommy had latched onto him. Tommy's head rested against his thigh. Carrie pressed the side of her body tightly against his. He stood tall, towering over them like their protector, with an old musty trench coat draped over their heads.

At that moment, Ezekiel felt more wanted and needed and part of another's life than he had since the night before Tom went back over to the war, the night Tom had finally confessed what had troubled him since he got the call to re-deploy. "I don't want to kill. I don't want to do it. And I don't want to die in this pathetic war," he had whispered across the pillow to Ezekiel.

"Don't go," Ezekiel urged him. "Just don't go."

Two hours later, Ezekiel hugged his partner of ten years goodbye at the Annapolis Army Reserves base in Maryland, not twenty miles from their home in Arlington. He had tried, unsuccessfully, to hold back tears.

Standing in front of the burning farmhouse, tethered to Ezekiel, little Tommy was mystified by the fire—more intrigued and mesmerized than frightened.

Carrie securely held on to Tommy's shoulder and, looking up at Ezekiel, asked, "How did this happen?"

"I don't know, but we're safe now."

"One minute there was that argument, and that was it, we were going to leave. Next, you and the old man plow through the room and then the house started burning down. Just like that."

Ezekiel listened to Carrie without really hearing her. Tom's house—the place that had nurtured his partner's joy as well as his pain—was vanishing before their eyes. Ezekiel thought he should feel sad about it, but he just couldn't get there. He looked again at Tom's mother. Her sorrow did fill him, however. After all, her house, life history, family's memories—all of it was disappearing before her.

Nevertheless, thoughts of Tom contradicted his empathy for the old woman. He imagined that Tom, with his square jaw and cock-sure smile, perhaps watching from another dimension, approved of the fire. Although Tom had glorified the farm when recounting memories, and only told Ezekiel a small portion of his childhood misfortunes, Ezekiel knew his partner well enough to read between the lines and hear the unspoken misery behind all the stories, even the good ones. He might not have known the details, yet he understood there were real reasons why Tom never wanted to return.

Tom hated this place and now it was burning to the ground.

Ezekiel glanced down at Tommy standing by his leg. The boy had begun to fidget, tugging the fabric of Ezekiel's pants and looking around at the scene in wonder. A mixture of inquisitiveness, weariness and excitement spread across his face. Ezekiel was amazed at how much the boy actually looked like his father.

And then the boy picked up Ezekiel's knapsack as if he were ready to leave.

Before Julian could stop the car, Melanie jumped out of the passenger side door. When she was gone, he leaned across the vacant passenger seat, pulled the door closed and sped down Quinns Way, leaving her and the fire behind.

Melanie ran up the driveway shouting, "Jesus Christ, Aunt Casey, where are you?" None of the figures hidden under the coats and umbrellas responded, and none looked familiar. "Auntie!" she yelled, imagining her slow-moving aunt dead in the fire. "Hello, hello!" she shouted frantically.

She feared the people in the driveway were the neighbors from the newly-built subdivision in the old haying fields on the other side of the fence, and that they had gathered to watch a tragedy unfold—to watch her family die.

Elizabeth, huddled under an umbrella, one arm slid tightly around her mother's waist, glanced over her shoulder. Recognizing her cousin in the light of the flames, she shouted, alarmed, "Melanie!" then, switched her tone to concern, "Where have you been?"

Mrs. Hubbard broke free from Elizabeth and, opening her arms, welcomed Melanie. "Thank God, child, you're safe." She moved out from under the protection of the umbrella and embraced her niece. She brushed Melanie's face, then pressed her lips deeply into her cheek and kept them there.

As Mrs. Hubbard kissed Melanie, she briefly escaped the incomprehensible circumstances unfolding around her. Life had prepared her to understand certain things—Father Hilliard having his way with her, her husband's violent tendencies, her niece's drunkenness and even her son's tragic death as a soldier. She understood these things as if they were almost expected. But watching the house burn, the home she was born and raised in, brought her children up in, watched a grandfather and a husband die in, this was unfathomable. This challenged everything her life experience had taught her. Now, temporarily dismissing this unintelligible event, she focused on concern for Melanie, who she held tightly, even as she smelled the sweet perfume of alcohol on her breath. "You're safe, child. You're okay."

Relieved, Melanie sighed. Moments before, when she had first glimpsed the chimney flames from the passenger seat of Julian's car, she feared more than anything that her aunt's unconditional love would no longer be there. Now certain of her aunt's safety, Melanie controlled her enthusiasm and tried to sound strong. "You're okay? What happened?"

Mrs. Hubbard squeezed Melanie's cheeks. "Yes, I am fine. Thank God—so are you. Thank God you left earlier. Jim told me—" She caught herself and proceeded slowly as if adding up a column of numbers. "Father Hilliard told me that he had seen you leave with that Julian—"

Looking into her niece's face, Mrs. Hubbard's expression changed from relief to disbelief. Her complexion cleared of blood and she stopped breathing.

"Father Hilliard—" she whispered so low her voice was inaudible.

Red, blue and white lights began to spin through the air. Fire trucks, police cars and pickup trucks suddenly clogged the road and driveway. Men uncoiled fire hoses and gathered in tee-shirts, boots and slickers. Their presence turned the Hubbard's private affair into a public event.

Mrs. Hubbard felt dizzy and light-headed. She turned from Melanie and grabbed Elizabeth's arm. "He's still in there."

"Who?" Elizabeth demanded.

Firemen trudged around them.

A fire hose slammed into Mrs. Hubbard's ankle, knocking her off balance. She stumbled and caught the sleeve of a firemen's coat. "He's still in there. Do something!" she shouted through the noise.

The fireman brushed her off his sleeve. "Everyone's out," he exclaimed and continued toward the house.

"No, no," she shouted and began to frantically wave her arms over her head. She wanted the firefighters to leave the fire and pay attention. "My God, listen to me!" she yelled, competing against the roar of the trucks and the fire.

Mistaking the old woman's urgency for an injury, two firefighters advanced toward Mrs. Hubbard.

Elizabeth, frightful of her mother's state of mind and concerned for her safety, stepped between the firefighters and her mother.

Mrs. Hubbard pushed her daughter aside and pointed a bony finger to the second floor. "Father Hilliard is still in the house!"

Chapter Forty-One

At some point during the height of the fire, it stopped raining. A three quarter moon was now pushing out from behind the clouds. The firefighters rigged up several large floodlights. Their halogen bulbs illuminated the smoldering rubble inside the remaining walls of the farmhouse. Because the roof had collapsed, the place looked like it had burned from the inside out. The two far sidewalls and much of the kitchen remained. But the front and the back walls above the first floor were gone. Remarkably, the chimney stood alone in the middle.

On Quinns Way, returning to the Hubbard's to pick up Neil, whom he was to drive to the airport, Ted Dorsey was blocked by the arrival of several television news crews.

Drivers were moving vans forward and backwards before aligning with the side of the road to park. A fire truck pulled out of the driveway. Its headlights blinded Ted before passing him on his driver's side. A police officer waved him on and he drove past a line of idling vehicles. A bright wall of light stretched above them.

It was as if he'd stumbled upon a carnival. He stopped a little further up the road in the darkness and parked in the same spot he had earlier in the day, just behind Father Hilliard's car. As he looked up at the commotion, a sickening tension pulled at the back of his throat like a sob. Tom Hubbard's house had burned down. He sat still for a moment and, folding his hands together, prayed to God that no one was hurt in the fire. Once out of the car he started across the street.

The police officer in the road recognized Ted from their children's kindergarten programs and shouted, "Not a time to be visiting."

Ted waved a hand over his head and shouted back, "I'm picking someone up."

His voice weighed heavy with the guilt he felt at having left Neil Bingham behind at the reception. He had only gone home with Shelly to help put their children to bed. He had planned to come back all along. The thought that something might have happened to Neil, or anyone at the reception, made Ted tremble.

In the driveway, Ted walked past more fire trucks and an ambulance. Disbelief challenged him again when he reached the demarcation of yellow police tape. The remnants of the house were bathed in bright light. Like a heart patient on an operating table, the chest of the house was split wide open.

To his immediate left, two rescue workers prepared to enter the smoldering ruins. They fixed breathing apparatus to their backs. Next to them, an ambulance attendant anticipated the worst and readied a stretcher.

Off to the right of the driveway, Ted spotted Billy and Jeannine Quinn and, with some relief, Neil Bingham. Beyond them, at the edge of the floodlight's reach, he saw Tom's family. They were huddled together, Melanie, Tony, Jon, Elizabeth and Mrs. Hubbard. He noted that the boy, the black man and the boy's mother were with them as well.

"What happened?" Ted asked when he got within speaking range.

Billy and Jeannine Quinn, although once in the thick of the fire, shrugged their shoulders as if duped by a master illusionist. They knew that the family was safe, so their reason for staying was concern for the unaccounted, Father Hilliard. Each of them loved the man; he had baptized them both and their children as well. Like the others, they prayed silently that Mrs. Hubbard had been wrong and that Father Hilliard had returned to the rectory instead of napping on the second floor.

Neil approached Ted and shook with excitement as he spoke. "The place just went up. It was amazing. I stepped outside to wait for you, and suddenly there were flames shooting out of the chimney. So I gambled and ran back in through the house to evacuate it before the fire took over. Then I—"

Ted cut him off. "Did everyone make it out? Is everyone okay?"

"Well—" Neil paused, "Tom's mother says that your friend, the priest, might have been asleep upstairs. So ..." Neil let the thought hang. He wanted Ted to get the gist of what he was saying without having to go through the discomfort of actually saying it.

"Where is he, though?" Ted missed Neil's point. "I just parked behind his car again, so he's still here, right? I mean, is he okay?"

Ted had no idea he had just confirmed Father Hilliard's death.

Jeannine Quinn overheard Ted and erupted into tears. Billy pulled his wife tight to his side. His own eyes swelled with tears as he looked into the bright crest of light above the house.

Neil and Ted looked at one another as the

knowledge of Father Hilliard's death sunk in.

"How could God be so unkind?" Mrs. Hubbard dropped to the ground when Elizabeth told her Father Hilliard's car was still parked on the road. "In one day," she sobbed and curled into a fetal position, "all in one day—"

She heaved, rolled onto her side and let out a moan that was so deeply rooted in her soul that it paralyzed those around her and prevented them from reaching down and lifting her up off the damp ground.

"My God," Elizabeth exclaimed. "Jon, do something."

However, a strange sensation resembling a déjà vu or a recurring dream had drifted over Jon—*It's like I've witnessed these events before, cleaning out the house, hiring a caterer, the funeral, the limousine rides, the burial ceremony, the crowd at the reception.* Even watching his mother-in-law as she curled into a ball on the ground, weeping like an injured animal, seemed oddly repetitive.

But there was a new element, not congruent with his awkward feeling of dreamy familiarity. It was a sense of satisfaction stemming from the new knowledge that Tom had lived a full life. Ezekiel, Carrie and Tommy, whether they knew it or not, had introduced him to his brother-in-law. Jon knelt down beside Mrs. Hubbard and placed a hand on her shoulder.

Melanie stepped back from the family, hugging herself tight against a chill that seemed to come not from the night air but from inside. She felt nothing for the priest. *And why should I? After all, the man had groped me, tried to rape me.* She had only managed to stop him after kicking him in the balls. But watching her aunt wilt into the ground, Melanie didn't know what to do. She needed her aunt's strong, supportive attention—she even relied on it. The constant phone calls, including the ones she ignored, and the knowledge that her aunt was thinking about her even when not around—these things had comforted Melanie and made her sober loneliness tolerable. Now, the idea of playing the opposite role—of supporting her aunt—terrified her. Her breath quickened. And, watching her aunt's grief from a distance, she started shaking.

Her brother Tony knelt next to Jon and her aunt, delicately touching, comforting the old woman. Melanie wanted to do the same; wanted to show that she cared. But where she hoped to find compassion inside herself— and a willingness to go to her aunt—she found instead ... nothing.

How does Tony do it? Who in our lives taught him to do that—to touch like that? I want what he has—to feel sadness, grief, love, happiness. Hating that she was drunk, numbly drunk, she closed her eyes to shut everything out, and there, in slow motion, she saw fragments of metal fly through the air and crack the shell of a sandy-brown soldier's helmet. Her cousin Tom's eyes burst wide open with surprise. She gasped aloud.

"Jon," Elizabeth demanded, "help her up. Tony, can we bring her to your house?"

Mrs. Hubbard wrestled free of Tony and Jon's clutches and pressed herself to the ground.

This earth was hers. Her family had tilled it for generations. The soil belonged to her—it had nurtured her sufferings and now it yielded to her sadness. Like the dense root system of the hay-grass in these old fields, her family, too, had once been embedded into, and thrived on, this piece of land. In desperation, she grasped onto the scraggily wet grass, dug her fingernails into the soil and pulled at the roots. Tom was gone. Father Hilliard was dead, too. She had carried the burden of Tom's origin throughout his whole life. Tom was unexpected; Father Hilliard had forced himself upon her. Afterwards, when she discovered that she had become pregnant; she sought him out at the church and told him about the child. Unsurprised by the news, he calmly explained that God, through his actions, provided for her what her husband was unable—a child. She was to keep his role in the conception a secret and allow her husband to take responsibility. If she agreed, the child would live under Christ's protection—Father Hilliard promised.

She agreed.

They knelt together before the altar, the same altar before which Tom's casket had lain that very morning, and he blessed her and the unborn child, and, in God's name, made an agreement with her: If she vowed silence, Christ would watch over the child. For almost four decades she justified her denial of the truth by hiding behind this agreement. Now, with Tom and Father Hilliard's deaths, she saw that both her vow of silence and her agreement with God proved worthless—it was a sham. There was no protection. No one had watched over her son. Father Hilliard had deceived her, and his death here was God's punishment for his actions.

God, in his wrath, had punished her as well. He'd taken Tom and burned down the house. Now she needed to purge in order to save her soul. She needed to turn herself fully over to the Divine and accept responsibility for her part in the deception.

The two Hubbard brothers, who earlier had lurked at a distance, appeared at Mrs. Hubbard's side as if on cue to hear the confession. Like evil archangels they leaned over the old woman.

Ezekiel, seeing himself as the dutiful son-in-law, took a position next to the two old men and prepared to intervene at the first sign of contention.

"What do *you* want?" Elizabeth, too, wanted to protect her mother from the men's torment. "Jon, get her up!"

"Easy does it, girl," Peter Hubbard grinned. "We just want to help."

Carrie held her son close and moved him around behind the brothers. She felt compelled to stay, although on the surface, none of it—not the priest, the land, the fire—had anything to do with her. It was more than she had ever wanted to see of Tom's life.

Her son clung to her, speechless, motionless, watching it all. She could only hope that by staying she had not damaged him in some way. She should have left, picked up the boy and run down the driveway, gotten into her car and driven back to Boston. But she stayed. Stayed because as absurd as it might seem, the sobbing old woman on the ground, the two men on their knees comforting her, the daughter barking orders, Ezekiel playing protector and the two old brothers hovering like vipers were all part of her son—they were his family. She positioned herself and Tommy at a safe distance from the brothers and readied herself for whatever would come next.

Mrs. Hubbard raised her head off the ground. "Do you see? Do you see what's happened? It's all been taken away from me ... all of it. Because of my actions. Because of what I did to my poor Tom, my son. Why did I ever let him do that to us? And him, he's dead as well—punished for our sins. And he said nothing would come of it. That God would forgive us. Even this afternoon, sitting across from me, he assured me that God approved, that we had done the right thing. But it's not true. Tom's dead and now he's dead, too."

"Mother? Jon, what is she saying?"

"Don't you see, Elizabeth?" Mrs. Hubbard lifted herself higher and Jon helped her roll onto her side. She had banged her nose when she dropped to the ground. Blood trickled from one nostril.

"I'm gonna get an ambulance." Tony jumped up and ran toward the fire trucks and rescue personnel.

The television news crews had made it up the driveway to the line of yellow police tape. They were in front of the house, jockeying for position: *Tragedy strikes soldier's memorial reception. House of hero burns on burial day. Stay tuned, full coverage at 10:00.*

"No!" Mrs. Hubbard yelled after her nephew.

"Mother, something needs to be done. You can't stay here. Look at you, you're bleeding. Jon, help me. And you, you, too." Elizabeth motioned to Ezekiel and together they leaned down to lift up her mother.

"No, Elizabeth." Mrs. Hubbard struggled against their combined strength.

The three managed to lift her up while she cussed and protested, determined to say what she needed to say. "Just listen to me. That man, Elizabeth ... Father Hilliard. He was your brother's father. It is true. Your uncles are right, I lied. I lied Tom's whole life. I thought it would help him. I thought it would protect him. Father Hilliard said it was what God wanted me to do and I believed him. But he was wrong, and this, today, this is God's punishment."

Relief washed over her after she spoke. She had nothing left to hide. Her body relaxed for the first time in years; it became fluid, lighter. Exhausted, she clung to Ezekiel's arm.

Chapter Forty-Two

Alley Hubbard curled the end of his mustache. He wondered how his sister-in-law, whom he always thought of as weak, had managed to keep that piece of truth hidden for so long. Father Hilliard was Tom's father. Although he still hadn't heard an apology to his dead brother Edward, Alley felt vindicated by Mrs. Hubbard's confession. Since Edward's death, both he and Peter had fought hard to get her to admit that she had humiliated their brother. Based on their brother Edward's claim, over the years they had persecuted Mrs. Hubbard for rearing another man's child while married to Edward.

Their brother, however, had only told them part of the story. Only Mrs. Hubbard knew the whole truth. Edward had left out the fact that he found sex with women difficult, even at times revolting. He rarely touched his wife. Edward never spoke of this to anyone because he feared other men would question his manhood. So when his wife became pregnant with Tom, he stayed mum about the boy's conception, telling no one, not even his brothers, that a marital pregnancy was impossible.

Then one night, when Tom was just three, Mrs.

Hubbard, fed up with her husband's drunkenness and frigidity, confronted him. She told him he was "less than a man." He responded with rage and, to prove himself, he raped her. Mrs. Hubbard became pregnant with Elizabeth.

Relieved he now had proof of his manhood, Edward felt free to treat Tom as he saw fit. After Elizabeth's birth, he began to regularly beat the boy. When Tom approached the tender age of ten, Edward told his brothers that the boy was a bastard, the product of an unfaithful wife. Mrs. Hubbard vehemently denied the accusations, explaining that her husband was an angry, brutal drunk. Most of the town sided with her and the rumors of her infidelity were quickly hushed—until Edward died.

Upon Edward's passing, his brothers wanted his dignity and their family honor restored. They took the family to court over land to which they knew they had no claim. They simply wanted the two-timing woman their brother had married to own up to her infidelities and tell the world the truth: She had been with other men and then forced her husband to raise an illegitimate boy. They wanted her to admit that Tom Hubbard was, in fact, not a Hubbard at all.

Peter Hubbard let out a sigh, took the pipe from his shirt pocket and placed the stem back in the corner of his mouth. "Goddamn," he muttered.

Like his brother, Alley, he now felt sure that all their past harassment, needling and even court actions were justified. In their minds, they had finally gotten what they had fought for, the restoration of their brother's dignity and their family honor.

"I told you it was the priest," Alley Hubbard commented to his brother Peter, loud enough for everyone to hear. "Guessed it years ago." Placing a hand on his brother's shoulder, shook it reassuringly and turned to leave.

"You were right. Rest their souls, Tom and Edward, both of 'em victims," Peter said, slightly pausing before turning and disappearing down the driveway behind his brother.

Jon was the only family member who paid attention to the brothers as they departed into the night—everyone else was absorbed in their own thoughts. Even though the uncles had picked fights and been verbally brutal throughout the day, Jon wanted to call out after them and offer some kind of acknowledgement that they had all just shared a profound experience. But he knew it was inappropriate to do so.

"Mother?" Elizabeth broke the silence.

Exhausted, Mrs. Hubbard weighed heavily on Elizabeth and Ezekiel's arms. She needed to sleep, to rest her head on a pillow.

"We need to go," Elizabeth said. She had heard too much; she felt dirty, repulsed. Violation loomed in her crotch. A man who had touched her down there against her will was, in fact, her brother's father. And her mother had actually had sex with him! Then, willingly, she had bore his child and lied about it for a lifetime.

No wonder her mother had done nothing when Elizabeth, as a young girl, complained to her of Father Hilliard's touches. It had happened when she was six, twelve and again at fourteen. Her mother only told her to "cover up" and "wear more clothing." Apparently her mother was invested in protecting Father Hilliard. Elizabeth wanted to shower, to wash off the ugly feeling that now clung to her skin. She wished she were home in California.

"Melanie, can you drive? Where are you parked?" Elizabeth asked.

Melanie searched her pockets for keys, unsure if she had taken them when she dressed after being with Julian. "I'm parked behind the house, in the new neighborhood, near the old haying fields. But I think I forgot my keys."

Even if she had had her keys, she was too intoxicated to drive. Not just her aunt, but she, too, needed her family's help—Elizabeth, Jon, Tony and Billy, all of them. And with this realization, she hugged herself even tighter and began to weep. She wanted to live life differently. Before, when she'd left the old farmhouse with Julian, she had wanted her family to leave her alone. Now she needed them more than ever—wanted to be a part of them.

Walking fast, almost running, Tony returned from the crowd gathering under the floodlights, where he had gone to find medical assistance for his aunt. There, he had encountered over-eager newspaper reporters and television crews, and decided it was best to simply remove his aunt from the scene himself.

"How is she?" he said, looking at her with concern. "It's a zoo over there. The fucking news reporters are everywhere. They want to interview a family member about Tom. They're calling Father Hilliard Tom's spiritual advisor. One reporter even said that if they covered the story right tonight, by tomorrow morning this place would be a shrine. He asked if I knew the family. Ted and Neil were already being interviewed, so I told him the family had left, but I don't think he believed me."

Then Tony lowered his voice to a whisper to shield his aunt from his next words: "They found his body."

"We could take my car." Ezekiel wanted to help the family move beyond Mrs. Hubbard's gut-wrenching admission. "I could give you all a ride."

Though still ready to help Mrs. Hubbard, Ezekiel

wondered how different his partner's life might have been if the woman had been honest when Tom was born. *What would it have been like if she'd raised Tom honestly? If Tom knew his real father?*

Carrie and Tommy remained a few yards away. Carrie caught herself crying several times when she thought about her own lie to her son. *Was it really any worse than Mrs. Hubbard's was to Tom?*

Her lie was a lie of omission. She was deceitful without words. While watching the family gather itself, readying to leave, she wondered what was worse: a mother who lies, pretending that God sanctions her lying, or a mother who never tells her little boy anything at all—nothing—about his father.

She now wished they had returned to Boston after the burial. How to explain all this to a five-year-old? She realized she needed to tell Tommy about his father and the family as soon as the boy was awake enough to hear. *Tomorrow,* for sure.

She looked down at her son. Tommy held Ezekiel's knapsack and was sleepily rocking, barely standing by her side. The boy was well past exhaustion. To him everything must have seemed like a dream. Watching him look so vulnerable, she was uncertain as to the best way to proceed. They needed to leave, but she wanted to stay. After all, her son was part of this family, too—it was his grandfather who had just died.

"Well, something needs to be done," Elizabeth said, again breaking the silence. "Jon tell the police to just keep them away. We can't wade through with a million news crews asking questions about Tom. We've gotta go."

"Yes, we're going," Jon agreed.

Looking in the direction of the smoldering shell of a house, Tony saw several people with cameras hoisted onto their shoulders coming toward the family. "I'll take them," Tony said to Ezekiel. "I've got plenty of room in my truck and I'm parked close by. You, too, Mel—come with me." Tony spoke with authority and urgency. Ezekiel moved toward Carrie. He reached a hand out, wanting to reassure her that he would be there for her and Tommy, not only now, but always. But they were so new to him that he was unsure of how to say this, so he simply placed a hand on her cheek and asked, "How can I help?"

Her eyes showed appreciation. Then Ezekiel knelt down in front of Tommy. "How are you?" he brushed the boy's hair back.

Tommy jostled the knapsack. "This is yours," he said sleepily.

"And yours as well, I hope, some day." Ezekiel glanced up at Carrie who nodded confidently.

Tony and Jon, each on one side of Mrs. Hubbard, lifted her gently and guided her safely into the darkness beyond the floodlights' reach. Elizabeth and Melanie followed. Behind them, Ezekiel and Carrie walked with Tommy in between. The boy struggled a bit, but managed to carry Ezekiel's knapsack over his little shoulder. The short procession that made up Tom Hubbard's family snaked down the side of the driveway towards the street.

~~~

About The Author:

When taking a break from writing, Robert Price works as a cabinetmaker in Western Massachusetts, designing and building custom cabinetry installations and one-of-kind home furnishings.

For more information about Robert's works:
http://SlipperySlopePress.com/RobertPrice.html
http://RobertPrice1.com

www.ingramcontent.com/pod-product-compliance
Lightning Source LLC
Chambersburg PA
CBHW030922120626
46554CB00001B/245